Dedalus European Classics
General Editor: Mike Mitchell

Hans Cadzand's Vocation
(and Other Stories)

Georges Rodenbach

Hans
Cadzand's Vocation
(and Other Stories)

Translated by Mike Mitchell with an
introduction by Phil Baker

Dedalus

Dedalus would like to thank the French Community of Belgium and Arts Council England, London for their assistance in producing this book.

ARTS COUNCIL ENGLAND

Published in the UK by Dedalus Limited,
24-26, St Judith's Lane, Sawtry, Cambs, PE28 5XE
email: info@dedalusbooks.com
www.dedalusbooks.com

ISBN 978 1 903517 86 4

Dedalus is distributed in the USA by SCB Distributors,
15608 South New Century Drive, Gardena, CA 90248
email: info@scbdistributors.com   web: www.scbdistributors.com

Dedalus is distributed in Australia by Peribo Pty Ltd.
58, Beaumont Road, Mount Kuring-gai, N.S.W. 2080
email: info@peribo.com.au

First published in France in 1895/1901
First published by Dedalus in 2011

Printed in Finland by Bookwell
Typeset by Marie Lane

Mike Mitchell

For many years an academic with a special interest in Austrian literature and culture, Mike Mitchell has been a freelance literary translator since 1995. He is one of Dedalus's editorial directors and is responsible for the Dedalus translation programme.

He has published over fifty translations from German and French, including Gustav Meyrink's five novels and *The Dedalus Book of Austrian Fantasy*. His translation of Rosendorfer's *Letters Back to Ancient China* won the 1998 Schlegel-Tieck Translation Prize after he had been shortlisted in previous years for his translations of *Stephanie* by Herbert Rosendorfer and *The Golem* by Gustav Meyrink.

His translations have been shortlisted three times for The Oxford Weidenfeld Translation Prize: *Simplicissimus* by Johann Grimmelshausen in 1999, *The Other Side* by Alfred Kubin in 2000 and *The Bells of Bruges* by Georges Rodenbach in 2008.

He is currently translating Jean-Marie Blas de Roblès' seven hundred page novel, *Where Tigers Are At Home* for Dedalus.

Phil Baker

Phil Baker has written two books for Dedalus: *The Dedalus Book of Absinthe* and *The Devil is a Gentleman: The Life and Times of Dennis Wheatley*. He reviews for a number of papers including *The Sunday Times* and *The Times Literary Supplement*.

He is the author of critical works on Samuel Beckett and William Burroughs, and has recently published a biographical study of the London artist Austin Osman Spare.

Contents

La Vocation was first published in 1895; the other stories are taken from the posthumous collection *Le Rouet des Brumes*, first published in 1901.

Introduction

"Very beautiful and very Poe" was Mallarmé's comment on the poetry of Georges Rodenbach, and Rodenbach's work – like that of Edgar Allan Poe – is heavily concerned with the aesthetics of death.

Rodenbach (1855-1898) will always be remembered for his novel *Bruges-la-Morte*, one of the great works of Belgian Symbolism: published in 1892, it immediately became a literary sensation and established something of a cult of Bruges among the French Decadents. It is the story of a man for whom the melancholy of "dead" Bruges – with its deserted streets and its silent canals – provides a perfect equivalent to the endless mourning that he feels for his dead wife. Bruges offers him a lugubrious mirroring of city and soul, and this idea of mirroring takes a new twist when he sees a girl who seems to be the living image of the dead woman; after which events slide inexorably towards their fatal conclusion.

Bruges (with its "air of a ghost town") once again casts its grey spell over the protagonist in *Hans Cadzand's Vocation*, published three years after *Bruges-La-Morte*. Well-to-do and well-respected, Hans Cadzand and his mother walk the canal paths like a devoted but mysterious couple, "at such a funereal pace and so shut off from everything outside their own selves" that even the nervous swans barely notice them, or feel "the shadow of the couple in black stain their white silence with

9

mourning." The almost Beckettian elegance of this image – blackness, whiteness, stain on silence – is matched by an earlier one at the start of Hans's overshadowed life, when his father dies soon after his birth and his cradle is dressed in black mourning crepe.

When he was young Hans developed a religious vocation but it became more complicated with the onset of adolescence, when he found he had a particular feeling for the Virgin Mary. Sexuality is never far from Rodenbach's vision of religion, if only by repression, as in a memorable line from *Bruges-la-Morte*: "A contempt for *the secret roses of the flesh* seemed to emanate from countless convent houses" [my emphasis].

Hans's mother feared being left alone if he entered a monastery, and tried to match him with a suitable girl. What actually took place, instead, has left their lives blighted, although the situation still has its compensations – and the same could be said of Rodenbach's story. In outline it might seem to have some common ground with the world of Joyce's *Dubliners* – as a short but thorough study of an underlived life, paralysed by religion, family, and provincialism – but Rodenbach is a more extreme writer than Joyce: where Joyce prided himself on his fine tenor voice, like a singer of airs and ballads, the work of Rodenbach, once the reader develops an ear for its themes and motifs, is more like a fugue by a crazed organist.

Among the many quintessentially Symbolist motifs within Rodenbach – including silence, water, Woman, hair, mirroring, dead women, and roses – *eyes* seem to take on a hallucinatory life of their own. The large eyes of a seductive servant girl named Ursula settle on Hans until he can feel her gaze on his skin: "the strange, brushing caress, the tingling the inert canals must feel, at night, when the star-studded sky is reflected in them."

Before long these eyes of Ursula are everywhere. They seem to lie beside him at night – while her blond hair grows on the pillow like a cornfield – and they follow him to church. When the priest makes the sign of the cross with a monstrance (a kind of reliquary, used for the consecrated wafer or host) "it was a huge blue eye instead of the pale host... [that appeared] captive, behind the glass." When Hans dreams, the eyes become signals at a railway station, and a peacock displays its tail as a fan of a hundred eyes. Darting all over Hans like tiny spiders, and tickling him with "a thousand invisible tiny feet", these eyes – as much as Odilon Redon's *Smiling Spider* or *Eye Balloon* – demonstrate the bizarre and proto-surreal tendencies latent within Symbolism.

The French critic and artist Philippe Jullian linked Rodenbach to the surrealism of Magritte: "are not some of Magritte's landscapes suburbs of Bruges-la-Morte?". He made this connection within a larger comparison that included their fellow Belgians Ferdinand Khnopff, who drew the frontispiece for *Bruges-La-Morte,* and Paul Delvaux, whose paintings of dream suburbs and old railway stations, where nude women lie on chaise longues, seem to melt the distinction between domestic interiors and streetscapes; between the mind and the world.

Symbolism and surrealism overlap in the way they give primacy to mental reality over objective reality, and this in turn gives rise to a certain kind of space: Rodenbach describes the room that Hans Cadzand's mother occupies, all decked out in mourning, as "her soul", and her house has a ghost "drowning in the mirrors." The troubled feelings she has when she overhears Hans and Ursula upstairs (in "a nocturnal scene, as disturbing and moving as a play or crime") provoke another of Rodenbach's looking-glass images, suggesting the significance of all these reflections as an essentially mental reality: in her imagination "The scene was there for her in the way objects are there for the mirror, she had to suffer it despite herself, *to live it out in reflections*."

Rodenbach's Symbolist aesthetic – with its preference for the ideal over the real – makes him equally impressive when he writes about the world that Hans is losing; the otherworldly sphere of his religious vocation, where prayers "fill his mouth with flavours as delicious as a ripe fruit melting on his tongue." However mean-spirited and damaging religion can be in Rodenbach, there is an ambivalence towards it, a constant two-way transformation, like his freezing of "the most ardent tears" into "funerary pearls". Rodenbach's art is less concerned with social critique or realistic indictment – he is no Zola – and instead with an indulgent exploration of certain corners and essences within his own mind.

Again, however damaging the enclosed and cloistered melancholy of Bruges might be to his characters, he seems to understand it because it reflects something that remains essentially within himself. This is no less than we would expect from the poet who could write – in a poem entitled 'Aquarium Mental', within a volume entitled *Les Vies Encloses* – about the "intimate and submarine" life of his soul:

> Thus is my soul, alone, and influenced by nothing!
> It is as if in glass, enclosed in silence, entirely given
> over to its interior spectacle...

The shorter stories in this book are taken from *Le Rouet des Brumes* (Spinning Wheel of Mists), a posthumous collection from 1901. Frankly minor for the most part, they still offer poetic pleasures of their own, in addition to the further insights they give into a great writer, the Rodenbach of *Bruges-La-Morte*; into Symbolism; and into their times.

Bruges is revisited in 'The Dead Town', where it becomes a "Museum of Death", with a smell like a mummy's tomb and a general air of forlorn belatedness: "In the churches a stench of dampness hung in the air, of stale incense, of faded altar cloths in a sacristy cupboard the key of which has been lost for hundreds of years." As in the novel, where the city itself became a kind of character in the story and played its part in a way that we might now call "psychogeographical", the ambience of the place once more governs the emotions and behaviour of individuals within it. A pair of lovers – an artist and his mistress – elope to the dead town, but it dominates them with a deathly influence that proves stronger than love.

'The Urban Hunter' is an unusually lively story for Rodenbach, and it is possible that it's meant to be humorous, although – like nineteenth-century *Punch* cartoons – its humour might seem elusive to the modern reader. It is the story of a man who 'hunts' women by following them through the city, in this case Paris: he does them no harm, but he enjoys *stalking* them. Sometimes he makes a conquest, but more often the prey remains untouched, and he explains that there are many such hunters in cities, often with special tastes: fat women, thin women, redheads, and others ("Women in mourning have their connoisseurs, in public parks where their black crepe goes well with the dead leaves"). The sexual politics have not aged well, but it is an interesting period piece for its sense of city-as-nature; for its contribution to the history of the flâneur, and the sexual life of the metropolis; and for its depiction of our romantic fascination with people who are anonymous and above all fleeting, within the phenomenon that Walter

Introduction

Benjamin called "love at last sight".

The idea of women is a familiar Rodenbach theme: women dead, women hunted, and – in two of the more minor pieces in this collection – women pregnant, casting further peculiar sidelights on Rodenbach, his strict Catholic upbringing, and his era. 'Out of Season' finds a sense of "sin" in pregnancy as it details a pregnant mother's embarassment before the three daughters she already has, while 'Who Is It?' makes a grotesque and fleshy mystery out of Ursula the village simpleton – another Ursula, here a misshapen, bear-like creature – being impregnated by a man unknown.

Grotesque or idealised, there is something eternally 'other' about women in Rodenbach, and a sense of woman as a beautiful object underlies his poem-like story 'A Woman in the Jardin du Luxembourg'. It opens with a superbly Symbolist description of the Jardin, where the landscape becomes a state of mind, before the protagonist sees a woman and picks her up with an appropriately dreamlike ease. Even as they live together she retains her mystery, keeping herself deliberately anonymous all the way to her early death: she has to die, of course, like an operatic heroine or a woman in Poe (who notoriously said "the death of a beautiful woman is, unquestionably, the most poetical topic in the world"). Finally she becomes, for Rodenbach, like a beautiful portrait of an unknown woman, within a cemetery-cum-gallery.

Rodenbach probes his obsessions further in the story entitled 'Love and Death'. This stages a group of male friends talking about love, and seems to give the author a free-associative latitude of the kind that people were soon to find by lying on an analyst's couch. The discussion wanders through the idea of lovers committing suicide together; French historian Michelet taking his fiancée to Pere Lachaise cemetery; the erotic appeal of women in mourning; a sudden sexual liaison after a death; and more – and all because "love and death are linked by analogies, by underground passages..."

There is more confessional introspection into this theme of death in 'At School', where the narrator – to all intents and purposes Rodenbach himself – remembers that his young soul "fell out of love with life for having learnt too much of death." He blames the priests for drumming death and the fear of sin into him, and three stories in this collection are directly concerned with death and religion, including a quietly gleeful anti-clerical piece about the death of a bishop, with its ensuing debacle.

Rodenbach said he wouldn't want to live his life over again, specifically because he would never want to relive his schooldays with the Jesuits. Born in Tournai and raised in Ghent (he never lived in Bruges, although he had family connections there) he was schooled at the Jesuit College of Sainte-Barbe, where he was a contemporary of fellow Symbolists Emile Verhaeren and Maurice Maeterlinck. As members of the Flemish bourgeoisie they spoke and thought in French, rather than the community's more normal Dutch, and Rodenbach's cultural affinities were always essentially French; he experienced Belgium as a place of cultural exile, which must have made it doubly deadly, including his "gloomy" and "grey" provincial church school: "Those who went to school in Paris know nothing of this sorrow."

The dead bishop in the final story 'The Canons' turns out to have been keeping a bachelor flat and enjoying himself in – where else? – Paris, and Rodenbach went there for a year in 1878, working as a lawyer and writing to tell Verhaeren that producing literature was "impossible" in Belgium, whereas in Paris "one is in a hothouse, and suddenly sap rises and thought flowers." He moved to Paris permanently in 1888, where he was accepted into literary circles and regularly attended Mallarmé's celebrated "Tuesdays"; soirées at his apartment on the Rue du Rome.

It was during this final Parisian period of Rodenbach's life that his literary absorption in Bruges really rose and flowered. *Bruges-La-Morte* was the Paris literary sensation of 1892, and he followed it with *La Vocation* (now translated here as *Hans Cadzand's Vocation*) in 1895, and *Le Carilloneur* (translated as *The Bells of Bruges*) in 1897. This kind of immersion at a distance is hardly unknown – think of Joyce, minutely anatomizing Dublin in *Ulysses* while living in Trieste – but it is also quintessentially Symbolist in its concern with the richness and plenitude of absence: "The essence of art that is in any way noble is the DREAM," wrote Rodenbach, "and this dream dwells only upon what is distant, absent, vanished, unattainable."

If Rodenbach had mixed feelings about Bruges, Bruges had similarly mixed feelings about him, and his morbid, melancholy and backward-looking vision of the city was resented by some of its inhabitants. In 1899 there was a suggestion that Bruges should have a statue of Rodenbach, but the good burghers of the town rejected it: instead they erected a statue to British guidebook writer James Weale, author of the tourist guide *Bruges et ses environs*.

Rodenbach has his final memorial in Paris. He hated provincial Belgian cemeteries (where his school walks always terminated, "so desolate in that austere province which had never acquired the art of decorating tombs") so it was fortunate that he should have ended up in the beautiful Parisian necropolis of Père Lachaise, where his grave has a remarkable statue by the sculptor Charlotte Besnard (1855-

1930). Extraordinary even by the standards of Père Lachaise, it features Rodenbach, alive in death, his skin copper-green as he emerges from his grey stone grave – reaching out, with a rose in his hand, into the city of the dead.

Prologue

At the same time every morning Mevrouw Cadzand and her son, Hans Cadzand, made their way back from eight-o'clock mass in the Church of Our Lady to Blinde-Ezelstraat, where they lived.

Bruges, the old grey town, was just waking. Passers-by were rare, only a few early beguines or the occasional peasant woman leading a dog-cart from door to door and selling milk out of copper jugs gleaming like patches of moonlight amid the fog. For the mists cleared very slowly, mist of the north breaking up, deathly pale morning twilight.

Bruges had the air of a ghost town. The high towers, the trees along the canals withdrew, absorbed by the same muslin: impenetrable fog with not a single rift. Even the carillon seemed to have to escape, to force its way out of a prison yard filled with cotton wool to be free in the air, to reach the gables over which, every quarter of an hour, the bells poured, like falling leaves, a melancholy autumn of music.

Hans Cadzand and his mother made a silent couple as they walked along the canals, taciturn. She was always dressed in dark material, he in black with something a touch old-fashioned, timeless, about the severe cut of his clothes, something self-enclosed and a little ecclesiastical. He looked still young, this side of thirty, with a nobility of feature which was dazzling. It was astonishing that one so handsome could be so sad: eyes blazing feverishly in a dull complexion and a turbulent mass of blond hair with a mingling of honey, amber and dead leaves.

His mother, already growing old, made her way beside him but, close to each other as they were, in reality they seemed very distant. The quais run parallel, but separated by all the cold water of the canals, and they too seemed each to be pursuing reflections without mixing them. Between them was a great, mournful mystery, cold and impenetrable as the water itself. What could it be? Public curiosity was aroused. As they passed, people often spied on them from the stillness of their homes, from behind the tulle of the curtains; and, thanks to those indiscreet little mirrors called busybodies that are fixed to the outside of the window frames, they continued, as the pair went on, to watch for a gesture, an exchange of glances, a sign, the slant of a profile which might throw some light on their secret.

The enigma of this pensive pair seemed all the more inexplicable to the inhabitants of Bruges in that life had been kind to Mevr. Cadzand and her son. They belonged to an old family, they had inherited ample resources, but they lived a reclusive life, cloistered, humble, reduced to the bare necessities. They spent their income on good works, on charity.

What had happened for them to cut themselves off from the world like that?

Especially the son! His behaviour did not conform to what was expected, to what was usual for his age. True, his mother, for her part, had suffered a great misfortune in the past, being widowed after only a year and a half of marriage. But time heals all wounds, consigns such grief to oblivion, freezes the most ardent tears in the fine hail of funerary pearls with which tombs are decorated.

And then, Mevr. Cadzand had had the compensation of this

model son.

Even now he never went out except with her. He had no friends, no business outside the house. The women looked with envy on this mother who was always escorted. It is the great sorrow of all women that their children go their own way, leaving their bosom as sad as a country from which one is departing. But this mother had realised the mother's dream. She was entirely devoted to her son. Her son was entirely devoted to her.

But it was precisely that which seemed strange. Why, being so united, did they appear to be so unhappy?

Without suspecting that they were attracting attention, that all eyes, lacking occupation in this dead town, were fixed on them, they continued to walk back along the canals after mass each morning, at such a funereal pace and so shut off from everything outside their own selves that even the swans on the canals, sensitive as they were, did not take fright, did not feel the shadow of the couple in black stain their white silence with mourning.

Part One

I

Great were the celebrations in the ancient dwelling in Blinde-Ezelstraat when Hans Cadzand was born. The old, blackened countenance of the façade was lit up by the white smile of the tulle curtains at the windows, which Mevr. Cadzand had wanted to look new as well, and bright, for this divine moment of nativity. The pretty swaddling clothes for the windows had been prepared along with those for the child. Oh, all those cool mornings, all those long evenings in the house during which this feast of white had been sewn and embroidered, hemmed and trimmed! Using only the finest linen, the flimsiest cambric, the mother-to-be delighted in designing, creating, enhancing with lace the garments that would enfold the limbs, the sleep of her baby! She had insisted on making the layette herself. She felt that she was the only person who knew the precise measurements, since she alone already knew the child that was to be born and could see its size within her. No other fingers were to touch the baby linen which would lie next to its skin. Made, handled by her alone, it would take on something of the gentleness of her hands, the motion of her heart, it would be like an extension of herself. Thus the baby, when it rested amid these coverlets and swaddling clothes, would think it was still inside her.

It was born one year, to the day, after its parents' wedding. A double anniversary! And a boy, an heir to perpetuate the fine name of Cadzand, which had for so long been held in such high regard throughout the land. The father of the newborn child was a worthy bearer of the name. He was a scholar who had obtained the post of archivist for the province so that he could spend his life surrounded by chronicles, charters, incunabula, rare manuscripts—flotsam and jetsam from the age of Bruges' glory, authentic relics of a great past which it was his pleasure to republish now and then in annotated editions and scholarly monographs. At the moment when the child was born he was entirely taken up with collating new and important manuscripts on Hans Memling, the naive genius of Flanders, concerning the disputed question of whether his shrine depicting the martyrdom of Saint Ursula had been commissioned by the wealthy burgher, as some claim, or whether it had truly been painted while he was being cared for in the Hospital of St John in Bruges, where it still resides, to give expression to the freshness of his dreams when he started to recover his health.

Thus it was because he was entirely taken up with his research on the great painter who filled him with such enthusiasm that he had the idea of giving his name to the child that had just been born. Hans! That pretty name which spurts up, not very high, then is turned down. Hans, a name hallowed in the world of art, a name to bring good fortune. The infant was christened with the name which, now ceaselessly repeated around the house by his father, his mother, his nurse, the servants—'Hans!' morning, noon and night, even in their dreams: 'Hans! Hans!'—had a freshness that made the continuous faint, moist sound of a fountain hidden in one of the rooms.

Oh, the joy of the arrival of a child, which is both the one and the other, a mirror in which husband and wife, who love each other, can see each other in one single face. The intoxication of starting a family! But any great happiness is a bright light, a challenge to fate to do its worst. There must not be people who are too happy. They would discourage all the rest, to whom life grants nothing more than unexceptional moments, intermittent joys, roses that have to be watered with tears.

The Cadzand household was too happy. The white smile of the tulle curtains on the old blackened countenance of the façade was too white. Hans' layette was too white.

A great misfortune befell his father and all the linen had to be edged with black crepe; crepe was tied to the cradle, like a flag at half-mast on the fragile barque setting out into the world.

Hans, completely unaware of the sudden mourning, made his first smiles.

It was one night that the tragedy occurred. Hans's cradle always stood beside the bed where his father and mother slept, the little barque alongside the great ship watching over its one frail passenger. It was his mother who had insisted on this vigilant watch. She was unwilling to entrust the child to its nurse during the night. These country girls are heavy sleepers, slipping so abruptly and so far away into sleep that she could well have not heard Hans waking up, have let him cry, get cold because of his habit of pushing the covers off, a gesture of the newly born and the dying as if, so close to non-existence, they were afraid of anything weighing down on them, immobilising them.

Mevr. Cadzand, on the other hand, watched over Hans punctiliously. She frequently got up and wrapped him in the eiderdown; even after she had gone to sleep there was still some part of her remaining, that tiny fragment of consciousness which is left and wakes us on days when we have to rise early to set off for some railway station or other.

When the child merely moaned softly, scarcely grazing the firm weave of his sleep, it was sometimes his father who, to save his mother having to get up, would stretch out his arm and rock the cradle for a second, imparting a slight swaying motion to the fragile barque, which quickly came to rest again as silence returned, having sent its little passenger back to sleep.

On that night the infant whimpered and Mevr. Cadzand, still embroiled in sleep, called to her husband, 'Hans is crying. Rock him a little.'

His father did not reply. Mevr. Cadzand, only half awake, said again, 'Hans is crying.'

Since her husband did not move, she felt for him to wake him up, to insist.

But what's that her hand has touched? It's like touching a block of ice! Finding her husband silent, cold, motionless, she gets up hastily. She takes the nightlight, which was fixing shadows on the ceiling like spots on the surface of the moon, and brings it closer. She calls his name, she checks his face, his hands, his body. Everything is frozen, everything is stiff, everything is over. Now there was a waxen statue stretched out alongside Hans's cradle.

II

The years passed. The child grew.

Every moment of the day poor Mevr. Cadzand was crying, 'Hans, Hans,' as she clutched her son's head. Oh, how she clutched it in her hands, such long hands, as if to enable her to enclose it entirely, such pale hands, which seemed to have turned into wax since the night when they had touched the corpse.

She clutched it passionately and full of fear, as if holding a precious treasure she was afraid of losing. Are a mother's hands not a key, a clasp to secure this treasure? They are also wings, they can extend, warmly surround, like a mother hen . . .

This duty of nurturing her little son had been essential to rescue the poor widow from the overwhelming grief which threatened to unhinge her mind. For months she had been subject to fits of harsh laughter, nervous tics, had been drawn towards a dear ghost drowning in the mirrors. The child alone had pulled her back from the edge of the abyss. Hans was her dead husband still present, the beloved she had lost after a year and a half of marriage. He had been so handsome, so good, so noble! Hans resembled him. As he grew up, the resemblance became clearer: there was his delicate mouth with the short, disdainful crease, his fair skin, above all his hair with its swirling lights, whorls of fairer hair in a mass of darkening gold.

Mevr. Cadzand adored her son, he was so elegant, and so

intelligent as well. From the very first months he had delighted
her with graceful charms, postures that could have come from
some engraving: amongst others she remembered how, when
he was very young, he had danced to the doleful melody of a
barrel organ that was passing. Clasping his gown in a dainty
hand pretty as a jewel, he had started to revolve, swaying in
time, like a hollyhock in a strong wind. The intoxication of
rhythm! Not long afterwards he had been undressed for his
bath. Hans was naked. And the barrel organ came back down
the street, grinding out some sad old tune. Immediately the
child had started to dance again and, not aware that he had been
undressed, had this time clasped his own flesh with his dainty
hand pretty as a jewel, creasing the innocent nakedness of his
skin as if it were the material of a gown. A heavenly moment, a
perfect little picture she had deposited within herself for ever,
a few touches of pastel to relieve the room decked in mourning
that was her soul.

Now Hans had grown. Already he was a little young man,
pale and serious. The time came to think about his education.
The widow sent him to a college run by priests where, from
the very start, he gained the top grades in his class, the first
prizes, the medals, the teachers quickly setting him up as a
model of diligence and good behaviour to his fellow pupils.
And they respected him with a hint of veneration, not simply
because of his success, his obvious intellectual superiority, but
above all because of the air of nobility surrounding him, the
fervent piety which transformed his face, encircling his head
with a halo such as could be seen in the college chapel round
the head of the Blessed Jan Berchmans. They were not far
from thinking that little Hans would also be beatified, perhaps
even canonised. What an honour that would be for the college
where he had grown up and for the city of Bruges, which has

always been a sacred fortress of the church.

The Catholic rites sent him into exquisite raptures. At high masses and benedictions, at Easter and Christmas, he would pray as a bird would sing. The prayers filled his mouth with flavours as delicious as a ripe fruit melting on his tongue; he counted the beads of his rosary as if they were the sugared almonds for the baptism of his soul and the Virgin Mary its godmother.

And the canticles from the rood screen, the thrill of the organ, which moved him to tears, pitching and tossing on its immense waves!

He closed his eyes, rose up with the octave then tumbled back down into a dazzling abyss. He was part of the music and the music was part of him. An ebb and flow of sounds sending harmonies, rainbows of colour, hosts, incense and all the blue of the sky rolling across the beach of his soul...

Oh, those Sundays in the church; and the Saturday meetings of the Sodality too, with, after the great swell of the organ, the gently flowing canal of the harmonium on which one glides, drifts along. Calmly meandering chords, a mist of notes rising from the keyboard to the statue of the Virgin, smiling in her velvet mantle, her long lace veil.

Because of his exemplary piety, his fellow members had elected him to the position of prefect, the highest dignity of the Sodality. He was enthroned in a prie-dieu, flanked by two acolytes, while the ordinary members knelt on straw-bottomed chairs. They wore a blue ribbon with the consecrated medal round their necks; he had a red ribbon, designating his rank.

In his religious fervour Hans had a dream that was close to his heart: to become an altar boy. Was that not a way of getting closer to God? He would see the face of Jesus in the host more clearly if he were kneeling on the altar steps, just as one sees the face of the man in the moon more clearly from the top of a tower at night. It was also a way of better serving God. He would play an active part in the holy sacrifice of mass, would present the cruets, carry the Gospels, would, at solemn moments during the service, ring the special instrument with twenty tiny bells which abruptly moistens the silence with a sprinkling of tintinnabulation, spraying the souls with its noise, like an aspergillum of sound. Hans was carried away by the very thought: he would be the one to sound the arrival of God, he would be the one to swing the thurible, creating all those little paths of blue in the air by which the eyes would make their way to the host.

He talked about it to Mevr. Cadzand: 'Mother, I'd like to be an altar boy.'

'Of course you can, Hans, if that's what you want.'

She was overjoyed. She could already see him in the chancel wearing the long red surplice and the pleated rochet decorated with lace. He would need two outfits, one for ordinary days and one for feast days with a silk cappa magna, a purple cape over the white linen. It was the college that would see that he was provided with all the sacred accoutrements and to see her son wearing them would fill the widow with pride.

One day he said to her, 'Mother, I'll soon be able to serve at mass. I'll have to shave my head.'

'Your hair? You want to cut off all your hair? Surely you're not thinking of doing that?' his mother said, disturbed by his sudden revelation.

'It's a rule, Mother. All the altar boys have shaven heads.'

Mevr. Cadzand's heart rebelled at the thought that she would soon see Hans's pretty locks fall under the scissors, that turbulent mass with its swirling lights, just like his father's.

No! No! The cold steel of scissors cutting into hair—it was

all right for a dead body. She had already seen a whole head of hair cut off, but that was her husband's after he had died. But to see Hans's hair fall would have been as if she were seeing something of him die, for our hair is part of us, our hair is alive. It would have been a kind of half-death.

Hans, not wanting to annoy his mother, didn't mention it for a while. But then, when his outfit was ready and a locker in the sacristy already had his name on it, he returned to the painful subject with great tenderness in his voice, cajoling her in such guileless, mournful tones as if, by insisting, his mother were dashing his hopes of happiness, were casting a shadow over his life, were preventing him from entering on the path along which he was being called.

Mevr. Cadzand continued to say no, giving herself over to sad thoughts and balking at the idea of seeing Hans somewhat disfigured by his shaven head. His fine head of hair harvested! The sun-ripe ears of corn scythed down! She could already see his little head bare as a stubble field, his hair short and dense, like grass that refuses to grow... However, she eventually gave way, but at least she was not going to let this treasure go to waste and insisted on accompanying Hans. How distressing to see his abundant locks gradually diminishing, his head gradually stripped bare like a sheep during shearing. But does one let a fleece go to waste? With an aching heart Mevr. Cadzand, in the gloom of the hairdresser's salon, bent down to collect the silky tresses. Hans, sitting at the mirror, was smiling as his face was reduced to an ascetic thinness, the slenderness of a pale ivory sculpture. He was not less handsome, he was different.

Full of apprehension, Mevr. Cadzand followed the metamorphosis: his head simplified, as if he'd been ill, as if he were in the moonlight...

Once the operation was over, she gathered up and bore

away all the hair cut off from Hans's head, a pretty bundle of silk cocoons with which she was going to spin out the gloomy days of her future. Instead of shutting them away in a drawer or a casket—which is only done with the hair of the dead—she even had the idea of letting them circulate, so to speak, letting them continue to exist outside, to be part of her life. She wrapped them up in an old piece of cloth; yes, she would make a cushion out of them, adding a little wool, a little swansdown. Weren't they the same thing? A swan, a lamb, a child, weren't they brothers?

The triple sweetness of three innocences mingling: hair, wool, down. A soft cushion that was never to leave her side, a little pillow for her days, a support to soothe her frail head and her frequent migraines. Now, when she rested on the gentle cushion of hair, it was as if she were leaning against Hans's face.

III

Hans's piety became even more fervent when he was made one of the group of altar boys. He felt that he was contributing to the ritual of the service, that he was playing a role in the great drama of the mass. How he trembled as he stood behind the priest, raising the chasuble at the moment of consecration, admitted to the privilege of being so close to God that he now felt that in the past he had only loved Him in absence. Face to face with the great sun of the holy sacrament, he lowered his eyes, dazzled by all the gold, the rays, the diamantine dove trembling at the top, dazzled above all by the host, the transparent unleavened bread on which, now and then, the glow of the nearby candles seemed to make the wounds of Jesus bleed.

Hans made the responses in a meek voice, his little silvery voice an echo skipping along beside the deep bass of the officiating priest, a humble brook alongside the river of the other voice, a feeble tributary mingling with it...

Hans was happy. And his mother saw that quite clearly when she went to the college high mass at Christmas to see, from a distance, her son in his new role as altar boy. He was so charming! Even his shaven head no longer upset Mevr. Cadzand.

It gave him a somewhat more clerical look, an angelic air. He moved forward so reverently, fingers together, at the head of the large group of altar boys going through their set movements round the altar in sinuous choreography: some holding a candle, others a palm or a thurible, a cross, a censer, all the subtle emblems of the ritual. They walked, they knelt, they intertwined in slow procession.

It was truly a heavenly choir, a religious mime-show, with gestures and steps loaded with significance, a sacred, hieratic ballet unfolding among the blue trails of incense.

Mevr. Cadzand had eyes for no one but Hans. Instinctive selfishness. When one has dedicated a candle and it is lit on the wrought-iron taper-hearse, one only looks at one's own, anxious for that one alone, for its flame as it falters, struggles, then flares up, outshining the others.

Hans was this fine candle that had been consecrated. Mevr. Cadzand followed him with her gaze, admiring, with a mother's naïve pride, his grace, his noble bearing, the radiance of his inner purity... The others have a muddy deposit at the bottom of their soul; even when they are pure, a little of the original mire settles within them and some always comes up into their face. He must have a pool of clear water at the bottom of his soul, for it was nothing but light that emanated from him, the reflection of an inner well in which the sky is mirrored and becomes aware of itself...

IV

And Hans's piety was contagious. With the zeal of a disciple he insisted God be honoured in his mother's house with the same assiduity as at the college. He was a day-boy, which meant he went home in the evening, at seven o'clock, had his supper and slept there. He persuaded Mevr. Cadzand to decorate the rooms with religious pictures, as in a presbytery. She too had been pious, in the past, but she had cooled a little towards God after the calamity that had left her a widow. Could there be a God, a truly good God, who carried out such designs? A jealous God! Did being happy offend Him? Yet to love helps one to believe and how can one believe if one can no longer love? Eyes veiled by tears can no longer see the sky.

But little by little her son's example had brought her back. They said their evening prayers together; Hans had asked her if they could. In that way, he said, their prayers would be more pleasing to God.

One single voice praying is like one single candle placed by the altar. Many candles are lit by the altar, there must be many voices, as many voices as possible, uniting, interweaving to create a great path of prayer up to Heaven by which God can come down. Thus evening prayers in the old house in Blinde-Ezelstraat had become a true little family service. The servants were present as well, kneeling behind their master and mistress at the back of the large first-floor room, which Hans's efforts had turned into a kind of chapel.

That was especially so in May, Mary's month, so bright and pretty. Then a statue of the Virgin stood in the middle of the mantelpiece, which was decorated to look like an altar, an altar of repose during a procession.

Warm evenings full of liturgical emotion: the painted statue smiling; the flowers of white and pink azaleas which, quivering like lips in the light breeze from the window, seemed to be joining in the prayers; then some relics: a consecrated boxwood bough, some taffeta posies under glass covers, framed pictures, silver-gilt religious mementos, some fine Brussels lace laid out like an altar cloth on the mantelpiece, all facing the mirror, which gave this artificial garden greater depth, making it recede into the distance of an enchanted grotto, into the infinity where reflections glinting on a pool vanish. Hans prayed, full of fervour. He was the one who recited out loud the litanies: 'Mary, mystical rose—Morning star—Tower of ivory—Gate of Heaven' and Mevr. Cadzand and the servants responded each time in unison, 'Pray for us.'

Indescribable moments in which one's life already has a touch of eternity!

And in the intervals of silence between the voices there was the sputtering of innumerable candles, whose flames, the window being open, flickered more than ever, sending huge shadows in waves across the walls, across the ceiling of the room, making it seem larger and crowded with anonymous figures in black mantles, kneeling, moving...

V

One day Hans said to his mother, 'I love the Virgin above all, because she's a woman...' He had given this answer in all simplicity, in all innocence, because Mevr. Cadzand had expressed her astonishment at his exclusive devotion to Mary, as if God didn't exist, as if Heaven consisted of her alone. This explanation, which at first seemed sweet and harmless, came back to Mevr. Cadzand several times during the following days when, her frequent migraine having returned, she was unable to go out and spent them dozing in her room, resting her head on the soft cushion of hair. It was so soft and soothing to rest her forehead on its warm smoothness. Her son was far away, in the dreary classrooms of the college, consulting heavy dictionaries, scarring blackboards with chalk. Concentrating so much on his studies he didn't even take the time to look at the big clock in the yard, to work out the distance the hands had to move round the face before the going-home bell would sound. But she, his mother, followed the game of hide-and-seek the hands on her little clock played. She counted the long hours, she missed Hans. At least she had something of him with her all the time: the soft cushion in which it had been such a good idea to keep Hans's hair. It was a sachet of fragrance, the constant companion of her solitude, the sure pillow for her periods of indisposition. It seemed to caress her through the cover, to give off an effluvium from the locks filtered through the cloth, a subtle perfume with the immediacy of a presence.

For minutes on end she would bury her throbbing face in the little cushion, as one does in water to wash off make-up, as Jesus did in the handkerchief of St Veronica, leaving his blood and thorns on it.

She needed its comfort at that time particularly because Hans's words kept coming back to mind to make her aching head a little worse, disturbing, worrying her: 'I love the Virgin above all, because she's a woman.' True, he'd spoken them without knowing, her dear innocent, still in the full panoply of purity, even in thought. But his words were a portent. The idea of woman was worming its way in. Her child was going to suffer under the advance of puberty. A critical point—and one to be feared! Perhaps his pious transports, his devotion to the Virgin, his ardent prayers, were nothing but the upsurge of the desire to love in his heart, in his blood.

Mevr. Cadzand contemplated the time that was approaching with apprehension. Oh, if only Hans could stop growing, could remain the artless adolescent he was! From now on his every step would take him away from her. And she had dreamt so much, still dreamt, that he would never leave her. Perhaps, since she was a widow, alone, since he was all she had, he would stay with her for ever. How touching it was, a mother and son forming a couple, living together, needing no one else for company. It must be so good to hear oneself called 'my child', even when grown-up, even when old. Several times she had mentioned this idea of never parting, of staying together for ever, and Hans had joyfully agreed.

'Because she's a woman.' Now these words suddenly appeared in all their menace. Yes, it was the love of woman that was the danger, the obstacle on which her dearest wish might founder. How it grieves mothers to tell themselves that, at the very moment it has occurred to them, there already exists a woman who is making her way towards their son from the depths of eternity. How it grieves them to think that they will not be the best loved, that they will not even be the ones who loved him most. It is the other woman who will be the best loved; it is the other woman who will love him most, since her love is a gift.

Mevr. Cadzand viewed this mysterious future with concern. If at least it was just one woman, good and pure, who would come to share Hans's destiny with her. But she was aware of the dangers, the pitfalls into which the free and unrestricted life of men leads them, the temptation of women—all the sinful women who are the mothers' enemies and who cause the mothers' faces to fade from the mirror of the hearts which carry their reflections.

Mevr. Cadzand feared for her son who, with his responsive nature, as sensitive as a hothouse plant, was more exposed. Fortunately religion is a means of protection, of diverting energies into other channels. Hans's mother was glad that they had cultivated his piety at the college and that she herself, with altars in the month of Mary, novenas, candles lit, rosaries recited and pilgrimages made, had further developed this faith, which keeps men safe through the fear of Hell.

Thus he would be armed against loose living and any future traps laid by passion.

Is not piety itself passion, but passion ennobled, sanctified? The whole of the Catholic liturgy, with its scenery and props, of which every one is an inspired invention, is enough to satisfy those suffering the obscure torments of a conflict between the ideal and sensuality.

The organ can embrace; incense is wafted like the fragrance from flowing tresses; then there is the miracle of love that is communion: first of all a kiss on the lips, then incorporation, possession, long desired, now consummated, in which one feels another being, who is a God, entering into, living inside oneself...

Mevr. Cadzand recovered her composure. What good fortune to have brought up her son in the faith, to have nurtured his piety! In it he would find, he would always find, a safeguard against sin, against the temptation of the flesh. Thanks to this deep-rooted faith, she would be able to shield him from other women, keep him with her for ever, realise her plan—and that without acting out of selfishness!

Did he not feel, in the church, an intoxication that was almost physical, the sole sensual pleasure that was not followed by sadness? And his passionate susceptibility, his sensuous, loving heart would find their best employment, an almost transcendent employment in loving God, in loving the Virgin above all, 'because she's a woman,' yes, the woman who, perhaps, would take the place of all the others, the only one of whom his mother would not be jealous.

VI

Now Hans was older, he had been through all the classes in the college, of which he was the pride, their model pupil. His teachers made much of him, would dearly love to capture him, a valuable recruit for the orders. Had Hans, with his quite exceptional piety, not been heading for the religious life since the approach of adolescence? There was no doubt that God had granted him the grace of such fervour as a sign that He was calling him, that He wanted him in His service. Hans believed this when he meditated on his future, when his teachers, in their frequent discussions with him, encouraged him to pray for the guidance of the Holy Spirit to obtain the essential, the decisive grace in life: to recognise his vocation.

A vocation! It is the great concept behind all religious education. Elsewhere one has only the world in which to choose a career. There one has the world and God. A truly momentous decision. In the one case, it is simply a matter of one's temporal happiness. In the other one's eternal salvation itself is at stake. The apprehension of the young faithful is understandable when the college priests, the convent nuns tell the pupils who are nearing the end of their studies, 'Beware, don't be in a hurry to leave. Wait. God may have given you a sign which you haven't seen. It is from among you that God recruits His servants of the future. He takes His tithe of the children we educate. Beware. It is less a question of God's interest than of your own.'

And it is true. Perhaps the only people to be genuinely unhappy are those who have missed their vocation. This word from the lips of churchmen can also apply to the lives of the laity. Even they can have a vocation: to be a soldier, a sailor, an artist, a doctor; to remain a virgin or become a mother—inborn tastes, an irresistible inclination, an instinct which would suffer if turned into other channels, forced into the opposite direction. How they are to be pitied—the enterprising man chained to a desk, the man with no talent who has taken up art, the woman born for family life wasting away behind the wimple of celibacy.

Even more so, then, when it is not simply a matter of choosing from among several similar careers, from among the parallel paths of the world, but to come out, from the start, on the side of either the world or Heaven.

Therefore it was an annual custom for the final-year class, as the school year approached its end, to make a strict retreat devoted to the important question of vocation. Each year, following lectures and exercises, several pupils would declare their intention of joining the priesthood or one of the orders. Hans took part with a fervour more rapturous, more exultant than ever. An outside preacher had been brought in for this retreat, a Dominican with florid, wily eloquence which wormed its way into the soul, like a bee whose sting still bears a memory of roses. How well he knew their souls! How clear his guidance, how sure his diagnosis of their inner turmoil, their indecision! How he piled on his words of advice about the choice of vocation, repeating that noble word ceaselessly, setting it alight in letters of fire to help each and every one of them see their situation clearly.

He mostly preached in the evening, when the college church was already shrouded in shadow. And he chose subjects that filled the imagination with salutary fear—sin, Hell, death—painting pictures that were sometimes cajoling, more often harrowing, evoking the effects of the fire on the damned. The little group of pupils listened, apprehensive, sometimes terrified, a distraught flock whose black shepherd is gesticulating towards distant flames.

He also gave special sermons on vocation, since that was the point of the retreat for the young men, who had reached the end of their time at the college and were about to leave. He described the world they were soon to enter, its dangers, its deceptive voices, its treacheries, its pleasures, whose superficial gloss quickly dissolves in the tears it brings.

Then, by contrast, he showed them the religious life, a safe refuge from which the passions and, consequently, the sorrows are banished, an oasis of faith, an archipelago of peace where God was waiting for some of them to teach them how to serve at His altars and in His pulpits.

The whole time he was speaking, Hans felt he was looking at him, that it was to him above all that this warning cry was addressed. His indecision was swept away, the mist enveloping his soul dispersed. He felt as if a great veil had suddenly been rent, as if the darkness inside him had faded.

An absolute conviction had shone forth. All at once his religious vocation, long dreamt of, anticipated, had become crystal clear, had appeared as if written in the air of the church. Glory be to God who had called him! He would go, his mind was finally made up—and since it was a Dominican who had come to preach at the retreat and had convinced him, it must surely be a sign that he must enter that glorious order himself. Yes! Saint Dominic's garb: a white habit and a black cloak, the colour of a seabird, to fly up to God! From that moment Hans's decision was irrevocable. He had been granted the grace of recognising his vocation.

He talked about it to his mother. Not straight away, but several days later, after the prize-giving, at which he won all the prizes. Now, having been through all the classes, he had finished his schooling, had said farewell to the college where he had spent his happy and pious adolescence within its white walls. What was he going to do? Mevr. Cadzand had not asked him, had not even thought about it, simply assuming he would tie his life to hers with no other desire than to love her and to continue his praying. He was sufficiently well-off to live a life of leisure, chatting, going to mass, reading, perhaps pursuing some scholarly study, continuing his father's work of throwing light on the history and on the great figures of the country.

Hans was aware of the dream of a life together cherished by his mother. She had often expressed it and he had always acquiesced, so as not to grieve her, awaiting the hour and the sign from God. Now God had given him a conclusive sign during the final retreat. It had suddenly been so obvious, a great light breaking, and he'd clearly seen his soul as a parlour where Jesus had come down to talk to him.

He made up his mind and told his mother, who burst into tears at his very first words. What was this? What more was God demanding of her? It was like the announcement of another death. She was going to be alone once more. Now it was Hans, pale from his confession, who looked like a second waxen statue after the first—that of her husband—that she had seen one night stretched out between her and the cradle. He too was already frozen, silent. Hans said nothing more; he had stated the will of God, simply, firmly, and now Mevr. Cadzand felt the icy cold of something irremediable.

'But Hans, it's impossible. What will become of me? At least wait until I'm dead.'

'God will give you the strength you need, Mother. It's a great blessing for us.'

'No, it's a great misfortune, Hans, for me and for you as well. You're still a child, you don't know, you can't know. Try to live first. Oh, how unhappy I am!'

Again the tears came. 'Hans! My poor Hans!' Mevr. Cadzand sobbed, repeating his name passionately, bathing it in her tears, her lips kissing it as it passed between them. She paced up and down the room, wild-eyed, distraught, repeating all the time, 'Hans! Hans!' as if it were already the name of something lost, a poor little bird that had flown away from her heart and that she was calling, trying to recapture it.

On that day Hans, upset by his mother's outburst, the violence of her dismay, did not pursue the matter. He prayed to heaven that she might come to understand, to accept the idea. Then he tried once more: he had to fulfil his vocation; nothing was more serious or important than to avoid a mistake about one's vocation. And his was plain, he had clearly heard the voice of God, he knew that he had been called. Could he refuse to answer God?

This time Mevr. Cadzand had thought it over. She didn't respond with tears. He should be reasonable, she said, shouldn't come to such a hasty, unconsidered decision. Of course she wouldn't do anything to hinder his vocation, but first of all one had to be certain, wait a while, go out into the world and only withdraw from it if one really felt one didn't belong.

He was young, too young. There was just one thing she was asking of him, as she surely had the right: to put it off for one or two years, at most until he came of age. He could continue his life of piety, his devotional exercises. She would even join in. They would celebrate Mary's month together again, with all its flowers. Was that not a sensible way of going about it, an excellent preparation for the religious life? If, after that, God was still calling him, then he should go, but until then she would not give her consent, and that was that.

She spoke firmly, repressing her tears, keeping her voice steady.

Hans was shaken. Honour thy father and thy mother. That too was one of God's commandments. And how could he disobey his mother, who was so noble, so good and so sad.

Oh yes, sad. Now Mevr. Cadzand was prostrate for whole days, overcome more than ever with her migraine, full of anxiety about a future in which the light of her hope was so faint.

What almost non-existent chance was there of seeing this religious vocation come to nothing, a vocation which seemed so fixed and which, moreover, had been prepared for by all those years of fervour and mystical raptures?

The widow reflected that she herself had contributed to the great misfortune that was facing her. Her own scheme had worked against her. She had rejoiced in Hans's ardent faith, seeing in it a means of retaining her hold on him. She had heightened his piety with the extra prayers after those in the college. She had thought to save him from women and from sin by devoting him entirely to Mary, but now the Virgin would take more complete possession of him than all the other women would have.

It was a love in which there would be no sharing. Mary was the one she must beware of above all. She had given a sign and her son was going to leave, to abandon her never to return, to live far away from her, as if with a wife who was even jealous of her husband's mother.

And to think that she had had no suspicion of it, not even an inkling—mothers were so blind, so sure of themselves!—

during all the stages of the fervour which was taking him out of her life: his first communion, the retreats, the months of Mary, membership of the Sodality and the little flock of altar boys.

True, she had had a sort of premonition when she shuddered, balking at the idea of seeing all his hair cut off so that he could have a shaven head, as the rule required.

But this first mutilation was as nothing compared to the other that was looming. When he had spoken of his desire to take holy orders, what had immediately flashed into his mother's mind—by some compression, concentration of ideas which can occur in the bewilderment of an emotional crisis—was just one thing that distressed her: the tonsure. Oh, to see now on that handsome, beloved head, whose covering of hair was already scant to allow him to serve at the altar, that wound, that permanent wound, as baleful as the single eye of God behind pale glass. Yes! That dead star, that empty clock face that only shows eternity, that one small patch bared to indicate the renunciation of all the rest of the flesh! The tonsure! That scar in the shape of the host!

That was all Mevr. Cadzand could see, even though its appearance had been postponed, all she could think of during the long afternoons when, prostrate with migraine, she rested on her cushion of hair, foreseeing the day when she might perhaps have to open it to add the clippings that had fallen to the tonsure.

But then the cushion would not be able to do anything for her migraine, it would be like a little death-bed pillow.

Part Two

I

'Will you come with me, Hans?'

'Where are you going?'

'To see Mevr. Daneele. She's expecting us.'

'No. I'm sorry, but I'd prefer to stay here. I'm working.'

Mevr. Cadzand didn't insist. She closed the door and the sound of her slow steps receded as she went down the spiral staircase. This happened every time she suggested a walk or some other harmless diversion. He only went out with her in the morning, to attend mass in the Church of Our Lady. Although her faith had become lukewarm since the loss of her husband, which had almost made her doubt the existence of God, she had also adopted the habit of attending mass daily, but that was more so that she could go out with her son, could spend more time in his company, because as soon as they returned, he would shut himself away, often for the whole day, in the large first-floor room where they used to celebrate Mary's month. The mantelpiece still had something of the look of an altar and the flowers before the statue of the Virgin, frequently changed, were always fresh, as on a new grave. Hans had made it his study, where he worked at a large table covered with books and papers.

During the few months since leaving the college he had sought something to occupy him, a task that was both pious and scholarly. He was working on a study of the Beguine convents in Flanders. He had gone into their history from the distant time when they were set up by the legendary founder of the order, Saint Béga, sister of Pépin, but he concentrated above all on the Beguine convent of Bruges, which still existed. Hans visited it occasionally, the only times he went out, heading for the green district on the edge of the town where it shuts itself off from the world. He spent delightful moments daydreaming under the elms on the raised strips of grass, following a cornet as it passed behind the windows, like a white bird frozen in the field of a telescope, praying in the chapel, where the names of former Grand Mistresses were gradually wearing away, together with long-ago dates, the fifteenth or sixteenth century, on the grave slabs with which it is paved.

He also spent several hours praying at home, reading his breviary every day as punctiliously as a monk. The study he was engaged on was simply a means of passing the time, to give meaning to his hours of leisure, which he saw as a transitional period.

Mevr. Cadzand was well aware of this and that he had not changed his mind. He had put off his plan, out of filial piety and love for his mother, but only for a few years at most until he came of age, as she had insisted. Even now he was living almost like a monk—morning mass, strict fasting, breviary and vespers, frequent confession and communion. He didn't mix with anyone at all.

Despite that, Mevr. Cadzand still lived in hope. Time was an ally whose mysterious power could wear away any plan. It subjects even our most vivid, our most firmly fixed ideas to a slow process of decoloration in which our minds reabsorb them, divest themselves of them, just as the flowers patterning a piece of cloth fade. Every single hour takes away something from us, brings something to us. Soon we only appear to be the same person. After a few years all the molecules that make up our flesh have been replaced. Is it not the same with the brain and the ideas which attach themselves to it?

And then, was Hans's religious vocation truly deep-seated, truly irreversible? Perhaps it was nothing more than youthful exuberance? Piety is a form of extreme sensitivity, a channel to release the excess of emotion. Religion is marvellous for that. It offers love without danger, pleasure without remorse. Infinity expresses itself in it. And what refreshment in the holy water of the stoup for fingers, brows and souls afire with adolescence! A passion for something so far off it is as if it didn't exist. No matter, it is enough to allow us to desire, to speak words containing something of love, as do all prayers. But let another ideal appear and the transposition will take effect. God has been humanised, now His created being will be deified, it is she who will be placed on the altar to be adored, prayed to, coaxed with flowers, embroidered with tears.

Mevr. Cadzand was confident. What Hans had said came back to mind: 'I love the Virgin above all, because she's a woman.' Unknowingly he had allowed his instinct to give away his secret. Should a woman come and touch his heart, immediately she would be the one who would be the Virgin, the one he would love above all others. But would she come, and from where?

His mother thought about it, but did not need to think for long. Little Wilhelmine, the only daughter of one of her oldest friends, Mevr. Daneele, had just returned home after finishing her education at the Convent of the Visitation. The days were long past when Mevr. Cadzand would jealously envisage spending the rest of her life with her son, who would not get married but would devote himself entirely to her, would be the constant companion of her old age. It was a selfish dream, for which she had been punished. Now he was thinking of abandoning her entirely, of leaving her for the monastic life. But at least there was a compromise solution. It had come to the point where she was not only prepared to accept it but desired it fervently as a satisfactory, even happy outcome. Yes, let him get married! She would keep some hold on him, she would retain him, even while sharing him. God, on the other hand, would have taken him wholly for Himself. That would be the worst, for him to be living for others and dead for her alone.

Now Wilhelmine, who had just turned seventeen, was beautiful, with that dark-haired beauty that is sometimes found in Flanders. It is a remnant of the Spanish influence in the blood, for the basic racial type is fair-haired. Are those with fair hair not born during the day? And those with black hair during the night? Certainly Spain brought night to Flanders.

Mevr. Daneele's daughter was an attractive girl, with a gentle appearance despite her black hair and matching eyes, eyes of dark velvet. She had a languid, pensive look, a charming shyness which at any minute could bring a blush to her matt complexion, the hue of the sky when dawn is about to become day.

Mevr. Cadzand liked the girl very much. She was also fond of her mother, one of the few friends she had in the solitary existence in which she had shut herself away since becoming a widow. And it had occurred to her that it would remedy the situation, would divert Hans from his monastic plans, if Wilhelmine should offer him her love. The ideal couple! Their marriage would put an end to all her anxiety.

That was why she had once again urged her son to go with her to her friend's. He had refused. But he had been there before. And he would go again. Mevr. Daneele, for her part, often came with Wilhelmine to spend the afternoon at the old house in Blinde-Ezelstraat. She had to pin her hopes on the charms of youth, the sweetness of eyes and hair, the mysterious power of the senses, the artless promise of lips, that red fruit which is like that of the Tree in the Garden of Eden.

When the two mothers were together, the same thought was in their mind, though unspoken.

II

Hans had recently been unwell, doubtless because of his sedentary way of life. He had lost weight and had changed a little, especially because he had let his hair grow while he had been ill. Once more it was a turbulent mass, whorls of fair hair with swirling lights.

The doctor having prescribed fresh air, exercise and diversion, he had decided to go out a little more often. His mother took him on long walks. She was sad to see him so pensive, his thoughts, as she was well aware, elsewhere, on his grand design. At most he would abandon them when she went with him in the direction of the Beguinage, crossing the bridge draped in greenery over the Minnewater, the Lake of Love, and entering the calm enclosure, where soft sounds emphasised the silence: leaves lamenting, a distant bell, a sparrow chirping—a sharp cry recalling a knife grating on a stone.

Punctuated by these slight sounds, the silence assumed an immensity like that of the sea around ships. For Hans, entering the tranquillity of this mystical sanctuary was like entering a painting, walking in spirit through the landscape of one of the Primitives. No sound from the world outside could be heard. And yet there were living beings behind those windows, free from passion, from worldly affairs, from the clutches of vanity and extravagance. Sometimes a Beguine would pass, so calm, with so little of the human about her, moving like a black and white swan, making her way towards the chapel, where canticles were unfolding. Hans envied her, it brought him back to his idée fixe.

'There's happiness here,' he said to his mother.

'That's how it seems to us, Hans, because we're just passing through. It's the things that are happy here, but these women, cloistered in their little houses, do you know what they think?'

'They have happiness,' Hans replied with fervour. It felt as if he was thinking of himself, was pleading his cause.

'Yes, a cold happiness, like that enjoyed by the dead.'

Mother and son were silent. In that moment God stood between them.

III

Often these walks, necessary for Hans's health, also took them along the quais, the streets beside the merry waters. Mevr. Cadzand preferred these strolls round the town. When they went out into the country and the houses were left behind, all that remained was the bell-towers of Bruges rising on the horizon. It felt as if their presence were not purely physical, as if at the same time they cast their shadow over Hans's thoughts, reasserting their grip on them.

In the town, on the other hand, in the maze of twisting streets, the bell-towers were not visible everywhere, often blocked out by roofs and other buildings. And there Hans seemed to take hold of himself again, to be freer, to liberate himself from them, from the reminder of his vocation. That was why Mevr. Cadzand, heedful of the slightest hint, of anything that might help release her son from his obsession with God and go some way towards giving him back to her, preferred to head into the town—all the more so because she often concluded her afternoon walks by dropping in on her friend, Mevr. Daneele. As if by chance, and with the collusion of the quais and streets of Bruges, which entwine, twist, turn and run back into each other like wool on the skein, they always found themselves, after many a detour, heading towards Spiegelrei, where the Daneeles lived.

It was a touching ruse on the part of Mevr. Cadzand as she pursued her plan. She had quickly noticed that Wilhelmine felt some agitation when Hans was there. He was so handsome, her Hans, especially since he'd been ill and had let his hair grow... waves of fire crowning his pale brow!

Oh yes, emotion was stirring in little Wilhelmine's breast! They were half-way there. She was taking a step forward; it only remained for Hans to do the same and there would be nothing between them but their future.

Every time she arrived with her son at the Daneeles', as daylight was fading, Mevr. Cadzand would resort to the same ploy. They would be shown into the two vast, communicating drawing rooms on the ground floor and Hans's mother would quickly find some pretext to take her friend into the rear room, leaving the two young people alone together in the other. The lighting of the lamps was put off until later, prolonging the sweet sadness of the thickening dusk, anticipating the promptings of night... Moments of unease in which the soul feels solitary and needs another to confide in. Wilhelmine was of a timid nature, she blushed easily; for some time now she had been blushing every time she spoke to the young man. In this half light she would doubtless become bolder, no longer blushing, since we only blush when we feel we are being observed.

During those twilight visits Wilhelmine would chat to Hans about a thousand charming trifles—the boarding school, a fellow pupil who'd written to her, a book she'd read, somewhere she'd like to travel.

'What about you, Hans, wouldn't you like to travel?'

She addressed him familiarly, by his first name. They'd known each other for so long.

They'd been children together!

However, Wilhelmine sensed that something had changed. The first time she'd seen Hans again after she came home from boarding school, grown up, transformed, with a downy moustache above his lips, he'd seemed to her a stranger who happened to resemble the friend of her childhood days.

How handsome he was, this Hans! When she looked at him now, she blushed. She had no idea why. It was absurd, but still she blushed. When he wasn't there, she wanted to see him, she felt she had so much to say to him. And when they were together, it was all gone, and all her courage too. He had such learning, he'd won all the prizes at college. And now he was going to become a scholar, like his father, he was working on a book.

'Is it true that you're going to write a book, Hans?'

Hans said yes, and no more. He spoke little, the way one would treat a younger sister who prattled on, listening to her while thinking of other things...

Wilhelmine chatted on, chatted as if emboldened by the gathering dusk. She wasn't afraid any more. She didn't blush any more. And in this chatter without lamplight the dark seemed to suffuse her words as well. Her voice deepened. Darkness can have a strange influence. It has something religious about it and makes one speak in a low voice, as if in a church.

Without saying anything intimate or confidential, since as yet she had nothing to confess, no love growing within her, Wilhelmine gradually started to lower her voice. And when people speak in low voices, it sounds as if they are sharing a secret—that is why all those who are in love speak in a low voice.

Thus it was that on that evening Mevr. Cadzand, who, from the other room, had followed the conversation of the two young people as it grew more and more muted, muffled, until the abrupt interruption of the lighting of the lamps, did not doubt that her plan would come to fruition. When she left,

Mevr. Daneele, kissing her in the wide corridor, was surprised to realise that her veil was damp, her cheeks wet...

'What's wrong? You've been crying...'

'No. It's nothing.'

Then: 'They're tears of joy.' And she hugged her old friend as if they had a great happiness to share.

IV

Mevr. Daneele, too, was happy to see the developing idyll. At that point she had no idea what Hans's feelings were. Previously her friend had told her of her concern, of her worries. But these dreams of life in a religious order are common among young men and women brought up by priests or nuns. Such a so-called vocation soon weakens. Would Hans persist in it? It was unlikely, even though he had so far given no sign at all of the beginnings of love for Wilhelmine. As for her, however, it did seem that she was smitten. Mothers have an instinct which alerts them to that kind of thing. There is a tie, a sacred tie from the womb, which is never completely severed. And when a child's flesh suffers a shock, even the delightful shock of love, it sets off ripples of sensation, spreading in circles until they reach the mother's sensitive flesh.

Mevr. Daneele sensed Wilhelmine's burgeoning love, deduced it from little signs: blushes, preference for a particular book, for solitude, a romance she chose to play on the piano, tears for no reason. Hans had not declared his love. No matter. For the moment Mevr. Daneele asked nothing more. Her daughter was too young. Should one bind oneself for ever at seventeen? She would prefer to see her go out a little, move in society, if only for one winter.

Social events are rare in Bruges, but every year the Governor gives a grand ball attended by everybody who is anybody in the Province. The old aristocracy was there, decked out in antique lace and ancient jewels from the glorious days when a queen of France could complain, at the sight of all the splendour, that nothing but queens were to be found in Bruges. Wilhelmine would have preferred not to go, doubtless because of Hans, but Mevr. Daneele, who also came from an old family, was determined to present her daughter at the ball. She wanted her to look her charming best. They spent a long time discussing what she would wear. Pink would suit her well, since she had a dark complexion. But white was more a colour of innocence, of inauguration. Are not the orchards white in April, when the trees make their debut? A white gown was made for her, décolleté, revealing her shoulders, the back of her neck with its adorable little nest of dark curls, her bare arms, slightly thin but with short sleeves puffed out, wings about to open. The gown was entirely made of tulle, a drift of gossamer, ethereal—a cloud pinned up! The true attire for seventeen! A harmony of white! Around her neck a string of pearls; white satin slippers; a fan that looked like a lily with fluted frills.

It was a great moment when the evening of the ball arrived and Wilhelmine finally saw herself arrayed in all this finery. She was flowing, like the curtains veiling a cradle, fresh as a white azalea. When she looked at herself in the large Empire cheval glass in her bedroom, it blazed as if it had caught all the moonlight.

Mevr. Cadzand had asked Wilhelmine to drop in on her way. She wanted to see her in her first ball gown. She also wanted Hans to see her, since he had refused to go to the ball, still the stay-at-home avoiding society.

A carriage stopped in Blinde-Ezelstraat. A moment later Wilhelmine and her mother came into the dining-room of the old house where Mevr. Cadzand was usually to be found.

She burst out in a cry of admiration: 'Wilhelmine! You look ravishing! You did well to choose white. And what a lovely hairstyle. Who did it for you?'

Mevr. Cadzand wanted to know everything, see everything. She made the girl turn round so she could look at her from behind, from the side, then from the front again, examined the cut of the bodice and the splendid fullness of the skirt, which swirled round her, sweeping down to the floor in pleats.

'Just a minute,' said Mevr. Cadzand, 'I almost forgot. I wanted to make my own little contribution to your beautiful outfit this evening.' And she went to fetch a sprig of white lilac she had ordered from a florist.

'They had to send to Nice for it, apparently . . .'

Wilhelmine took the pale spray from her. Delighted with it and very moved, she embraced Mevr. Cadzand and pinned the fragile flowers to her waist, where they merged with the fragile material.

'Hans must see you like this!'

Mevr. Cadzand summoned the maids to fetch him and they in their turn went into raptures, especially Barbara, the old cook, who had been with them for twenty years and who was allowed certain familiarities. She put her hands together, admiring Wilhelmine as if she were a princess in the procession.

Steps were heard from the silent staircase. It was Hans coming down from his room. He entered.

'Well then? Don't you think she looks pretty?' Mevr. Daneele asked.

Hans looked at Wilhelmine and seemed flustered, embarrassed. He said yes, mechanically, out of politeness. Then he withdrew into one of the darker corners of the room, without speaking. Mevr. Cadzand had started singing Wilhelmine's praises again. She reattached the sprig of lilac, which had come loose, its white petals like flakes drifting off from the solid snow of the tulle.

Wilhelmine turned her eyes towards Hans, saddened by his silence. She felt less happy, less white, as if Hans, as he came in, had cast a great shadow over her bright gown, had put out one of the lamps as he came in.

Mevr. Daneele asked what time it was. 'What? Ten o'clock already! We must go, right away.'

And they went, leaving Mevr. Cadzand in a sombre mood, disappointed with the scene which she had thought would help bring nearer the happy future she was striving to ensure. Wouldn't Hans, having seen Wilhelmine so charming in her finery, see her as beautiful at last, start to fall in love with her? Perhaps the virginal white gown would turn his thoughts to that other white dress she would wear one day as she made her way to the altar. The association of ideas can suddenly reveal things within people which they had never imagined were there. But the white had not worked its spell, alas. On the contrary, Hans had shrunk back, doubtless put off at finding her frivolous, seeing her as worldly and vain.

There was even more to it. In reality, when he had entered the dining-room he had been shocked to see Wilhelmine dressed like that and to have been summoned to see her. For a young girl to take immodesty to that point—and with the connivance of the two mothers! Hans had never wanted to go to a ball. He could not imagine that women could be so shameless as to wear a low-cut dress that revealed so much of their bare flesh: their shoulders, the line of their back, their arms and, above all, that disturbing swelling of the chest, the mystery of which he had never dared imagine in thought, and which made him lower his eyes even at statues and pictures. That day he had almost caught a glimpse of the warm valley, the pair nestling there. Standing up, Wilhelmine seemed to be rising, naked, from all the tulle. A woman's body, the trunk of the tree of temptation bearing the ripe fruit of the breasts with, doubtless, the eternal serpent hiding there, coiled round them.

Hans had shrunk back into the shadow, alarmed, as if faced with something that endangered his soul. For a long time the apparition stayed with him, haunting him with details of which he desperately tried to purge all trace from his mind...

V

One day Mevr. Daneele found Wilhelmine all in tears. She had thrown herself down on her bed and was crying, face down on her pillow, her hair falling loose in black rivulets.

'What's wrong?'

'Nothing... Leave me alone... '

An expression of mental suffering as well as of physical pain, of fear that someone might come too close to our sorrow, touch the sore, even to make it better. But a mother's hands have healing powers, as if they had made the outgrown swaddling clothes into lint with which they dress their children's wounds all life long.

Wilhelmine was sensitive, susceptible. Given the mothers' stratagem of meetings and conversations with Hans, it was natural the girl's feelings should be aroused by him. He had a noble countenance, and one so handsome that all the women turned to look at him. But Wilhelmine was hurt by his coldness. At the beginning all she wanted was to be with him. She would blush, but it was good to blush when evening was approaching and, thanks to the shadows, it wasn't noticeable. It gave her a feeling of warmth, as if she were being caressed by roses, as if she'd plunged her face into a bouquet. When he was there, she felt she was a different woman, she seemed to have found herself after she'd been lost, to have come home after a long voyage. And Hans's voice, so deep and with a sound that went on and on! It was as if she could see it coming towards her, going down inside her, awakening things that moved inside her, stretched, then left, going back to him. It was a harmony, an exchange, the mingling of smoke from two neighbouring roofs. First love! One's whole being in turmoil! The arousal of something unknown! A mysterious white rose that must be watered with tears springing up in one's heart!

After Hans left with his mother, Wilhelmine would feel unsettled. The hours passed slowly. The silence in the house was wearisome. She tried to recapture the sound of Hans's voice, to reconstruct his face, sad that its elusive contours kept slipping away. How frail is human memory, where solely the present appears and which does so little to remedy absence, only retaining as much of what one would like to see as remains in the depths of a mirror. She could just about recall his luminous hair, the sharp ridge of his nose, his general build; but the indefinable shade of his eyes, the line of his lips, ending in a little, slightly disdainful crease? Wilhelmine tried and tried, she had need of that dear face. She would very much have liked to have a portrait of him to help her...

But she didn't dare ask him for one, she didn't dare say anything to him. He was always so earnest and cold, talking to her as if with a stranger, or a younger sister to whom he had nothing to say. It must be because he'd known her too well as a child to be able to treat her as a grown-up now, as the young woman she'd become. It would never occur to him that he could love her other than as a childhood friend, that he could marry her.

Wilhelmine was in despair.

When she found her in tears, her mother didn't doubt for a moment what had caused her sorrow. A girl's tears—tears of love.

She induced her daughter to confide in her, then gently

consoled her, counselled her. She told Wilhelmine the things she had been ignorant of until that point: Hans's extreme devoutness, his old plans, his religious vocation, his desire to take holy orders, which Mevr. Cadzand had thwarted, getting him to promise to wait a while, to postpone it until he came of age. And that kind of resolution didn't last, would fade away, provided one spent several years out in the world.

'Yes, of course,' Wilhelmine said. 'When I was in the convent I wanted to be a nun as well.'

'So don't worry. Keep up your hopes. Mevr. Cadzand and I saw clearly how you felt and we'd both be delighted for you to marry Hans. He's worthy of your love, so no more tears, Wilhelmine.'

She flung her arms around her mother in an ecstatic embrace, her eyes bright, dried of the tears her despair had brought to them.

'Yes!... But what if he persists, still wants to be a priest?'

'That's up to you, Wilhelmine. Make him love you. You love him, that's the main thing. See that he suspects, begins to realise... Men mostly fall in love when they know a woman loves them.'

VI

Mevr. Daneele described the scene of Wilhelmine's sadness to Mevr. Cadzand. How touching! Two mothers colluding in the same goal, which would cure both their sick children. In truth their sickness, though seeming very different, was similar. One was suffering from faith, the other from love. But faith and love, are they not the two faces of the infinite? Both of them suffered from a combination of solitariness and fullness, of a need to extend and to exchange themselves. We have but one heart to accommodate all our loves—doubtless Hans prayed to God with words full of affection; Wilhelmine loved Hans with outbursts of adoration.

And the remedy was the same too. Each had to cure the other. But how could they be persuaded? The two mothers were uncertain and almost anxious, as they also were looking forward to this great event, the hoped-for marriage, to feel closer together, after so many years of constant affection, almost as if they belonged to the same family... They felt that on the day of the wedding they would become sisters.

Mevr. Daneele advised her old friend to talk to Hans about it, to probe, to see if she could find out. But she was unsure what tactics to adopt, her son must not suspect there was a scheme, a plan being followed. He would be less amenable to persuasion the more she seemed to be trying to influence him, to be encroaching on his future, to be reopening the question of his vocation which had been settled between them. No doubt things would sort themselves out, it was preferable to let them take their course. Young hearts understood each other instinctively, without having to spell things out. One day there would be something subtly different about the moment or her tone of voice, and Wilhelmine would do more with one word than the two mothers could do with all their stratagems and long speeches.

That was Mevr. Cadzand's view, that they had to put all their hope in Wilhelmine, in her charm, in the mysterious, infectious power of love. In fact—and without confessing this to her friend—deep down inside she felt that all she could hope for was a miracle. She had been spying on her son and was well aware that his devotion was still intact, that he was already leading a monastic life, that he had found it hard to resign himself to putting off his plan and had only done so out of filial affection and to keep his promise. But he continued to live in the world as if he were in exile, ticking off his monotonous days, employing them in some research work that aroused no enthusiasm, entirely turned towards God, his melancholy features only softened by a modicum of content when they went to church, when the organ resounded, the services unfolded. The rest of the time he seemed to be waiting.

As for Wilhelmine, he responded to her with feelings of disquiet, unease, as if to someone who was too profane, especially since the evening when she had come in her ball gown.

Mevr. Cadzand realised all this, but still she hoped. Do we not continue to hope for what we long for right to the very end?

VII

A Sunday afternoon in winter. Mevr. Cadzand and Mevr. Daneele had agreed to go on an excursion to Damme. Despite his reclusive habits, Hans had to join them because his health was still poor and the doctor had repeated his prescription of walks and fresh air. It had frozen during the last few days, especially the previous night, which was why they had planned this walk along the canal leading to the little dead town. They knew how picturesque it was along the banks when everything was frozen: stalls selling punch and pancakes; children skipping round and round, chanting, 'The fish are warm beneath the white floor of ice; we are warm running about on top'; and skaters come from nearby Holland, who stand out with their rolling rhythm, a poised swaying, a way of swinging their bodies, balancing on one leg, each in turn, like a boat rocking to and fro on a wave. For the Dutch skating is like dancing.

The two families, who had met at Mevr. Daneele's, on Spiegelrei, set off along the line of canals leading to Damme Gate. The sun was shining brightly. The intense cold set their pulses racing and made them lively and merry. The two mothers chattered. Wilhelmine was in a talkative mood as well and Hans was interested to see what was going on in the streets.

The occasional skater had even ventured onto the canals within the town, frozen as they were in a thick layer of ice.

It produced a strange effect: with a quai on either side of the frozen canal, it was like three parallel streets, a triptych with the solidified canal forming the slightly recessed central panel.

Here and there, alongside the walkers on the quai, were skaters slicing through the empty space. It was as if there were, in the middle, a higher life form, more agile, more aerial, endowed with an extra sense, still half human but already half angel, which, on the surface of the ice, was taking off, appeared to be flying.

The group had reached Damme Gate and the green, the olive green, of the melancholy embankments. They turned for a last look at the town crisply outlined in the sun. Oh, the tone of the sunlight flooding Bruges on a frosty afternoon—the tone of candles on a virgin's catafalque—the sunbeams over the winter town, the veneer of pale russet on the ice, like the patina on old paintings which here gave the air, the canals and the streets the colour and something of the atmosphere of a museum! Once they had left the town and were out in the open country, following the tree-lined canal, Wilhelmine took it into her head to go down onto the ice for a while. The two mothers had misgivings...

But Hans, in a decidedly lighter, almost merry mood, went along with it. He held her by the hand to help her down the grassy bank and, impelled by the slope, they ran down together. Wilhelmine was enjoying herself and was amazed at the ice, it was so different in places. Is it some chemistry of the air which affects it, taints it, mixing fleeting tones into the white—cloudy sheets of molten lead, veins of blue? Or was it caused by reflections retained by the water, skyscapes absorbed by it and showing through?

Further on and all of a sudden, the ice was quite dark. An ice-skate had passed over it.

'Oh look, it's like chalk on a slate!' Wilhelmine said.

Hans smiled, enchanted by the appropriateness of the image, and complimented her on it.

Wilhelmine felt a little thrill inside. Hans was unrecognisable, he seemed less self-enclosed, less morose. It was the first time he'd talked to her like that. Was he starting to feel something for her?

She had been making an effort for so long now! On that day too she'd chosen her outfit just for him. She looked ravishing in her velvet hat and the dark furs mingling with her hair of the same colour. And her lips alongside the furs, very red from the cold, aroused thoughts of daring deeds, of the hunt and of blood, as if her mouth were a wound that went with the animal hair.

Wilhelmine was walking with the lithe steps of an Amazon, emboldened by the frost that clings to the body, sheathing it in armour, inspiring heroism. She felt like a different woman. Was it really because of the weather, which has such an influence on us, making us lethargic in the heat, fortified in the cold, depressed in the rain? Perhaps it was also because of Hans and the pleasant things he'd said, so unexpected, which had suddenly given her a strength, a zest which made her feel ready to take on the whole world.

However, the ice on the canal being cold to the feet, Hans decided to go back up onto the path. He helped Wilhelmine climb the embankment, where the grass was slippery with frost, pulling her up by the hand while the two mothers smiled to see their graceful ascent.

Wilhelmine had trembled to feel her hand grasped by Hans's hand, a firm hand, truly, proving that his health was only poor because of the kind of life he chose to lead.

Oh that grip, which for him was purely mechanical, with

nothing of his soul going down into his fingers, how disturbing it was to Wilhelmine, an exquisite contact which spread through her whole being, as if he'd crushed a fragrant fruit in her palm, emptied a phial, and the juice, the aroma, had flowed into every one of her members, entirely permeating her blood.

She would have liked to stay like that, her hand in his, for the rest of the walk, for the rest of her life.

But Hans had only taken hold of it to help her back up the slope. Now they had rejoined their mothers and were once more in a group, walking towards Damme, whose huge tower was already looming up ahead, etched black against the pale screen of the sky.

Wilhelmine fell silent and pensive. She felt that something new had happened between her and Hans, that something decisive was about to happen. She had never loved him so much as she did that day and never until that day had she hoped he might love her as well. She had a kind of premonition, the feeling the hour was going to strike with a different ring. Suddenly she remembered—why at that precise moment?— what her mother had said on the day she'd found her in tears: 'Men mostly fall in love when they know a woman loves them.'

But then and later she had not dared to tell Hans she loved him. Now she felt she would have no difficulty confessing it to him, and that straight away. The moment that must come, always comes. Events come to pass of their own accord. In matters of love above all. The white rose-tree of first love—the flower is about to fall and we think we are gathering it when it is the rose itself that is shedding its petals.

Thus it was that Wilhelmine could be both very calm and very disturbed, quite focused at the centre of complete confusion. What was calm and focused was her immutable destiny, which was about to unfold inside her and without her.

Everything would happen according to the logic of the mystery; if not, why was she looking for a chance to be alone with Hans to confess her love to him?

Before this she had thought that she could have told everyone about it, apart from Hans himself. Now she felt that she could only speak about it to him, and to him alone— not even to her mother who, after all, knew about it and had advised her what to do. The time of fulfilment had come and the procedure was no longer governed by her own volition, but by destiny.

So Wilhelmine knew she was going to speak to Hans and that her future life depended on it. She was ready. She was waiting.

All at once they saw a sleigh approaching on the frozen canal. It was coming from Holland, pulled by a horse that was trotting along the ice as if on a road. It was slim and swift, outstripping the wind, spattering the silence with the metallic jingling of its little bells.

Mevr. Cadzand and Mevr. Daneele, Hans and Wilhelmine had stopped to watch the picturesque equipage. Sitting on the bench seat was a young woman, pretty, her pink face wrapped up in one of those bonnets with wings they wear in the border villages, the starched cloth and the lace attached with jewellery and gold discs and spirals. Behind her, standing up holding the long reins, was a countryman of stately bearing, clean-shaven and weather-beaten. He bent over her neck, warming it with the burning embers of his lips. A handsome couple, newly-weds perhaps, who looked as if they were going on their honeymoon in the sleigh gaily painted like a boat.

Their mothers had walked on, but Hans and Wilhelmine stopped to watch the smart, swift equipage disappearing along the ice a while longer.

Thus the two young people were alone.

Wilhelmine said, 'They must be newly-weds.'

'Why do you say that?'

'Because they look so happy.'

Hans made no reply. There was silence. But Wilhelmine was resolved, as if a voice within were commanding her to speak and that the moment that must come had come.

She went on, 'I'd like to be in their place, going away with someone... '

Then, with an effort, 'With you, yes, going far, far away with you Hans, where there'd just be the two of us...'

Hans looked at her, surprised, uncomprehending.

'Oh yes, Hans! Haven't you guessed... all this time? I've been in love with you all this time. And you?'

Hans was completely taken aback. He stammered, 'But ... that's impossible!'

That struck fear into Wilhelmine's heart. Had he really persisted in his vocation, stuck to his resolution to take holy orders? If that were so, why the lure of an apparent change, those kinder words, that softening just now that had given her the courage to...?

She wanted to know, to clear the matter up straight away. 'Impossible? But why? Don't you realise that even our mothers would be delighted?'

'They know about it?'

Immediately Hans understood the long and touching scheme. Oh, this was the greatest temptation, the hardest sacrifice God was demanding of him. But he would not hesitate, he would not waver in his vocation, which was clear and irrevocable. He had given himself to God and he would not go back on it. But these poor souls he was going to make sad! He understood now why his mother had made so much of her friendship with Mevr. Daneele, the frequent meetings, the walks. And poor Wilhelmine was in love with him, so pretty and so sad now at his silence. Hans could think of nothing to say. They faced each other in mute incomprehension, as if there were a dead body stretched out between them.

Hans, however, was thinking, with the rapidity of thought one has at such moments, that for him she represented a serious temptation, the tender trap of Eve, who is ever the devil's ally, colluding in the attempt to divert him from his chosen path. Was that not what she had been already when she had come to their house, on the evening of her first ball, in that gown which had so offended him? Suddenly he saw again her bare shoulders, the curve of her back, her arms and, above all, the sinful fruits of her breasts, the forbidden fruit pressing against the tulle.

So he steeled himself and spoke, trying to soften the blow of what he had to say with a very sad, very gentle voice. But above all without equivocating out of concern for her feelings. No, he would never marry. He was going to be a monk and had only put it off for a while out of consideration for his poor mother. Wilhelmine must forget him. She was the sister of his childhood, she would remain his sister in the Holy Mother Church...

Wilhelmine was crying. When the two mothers suddenly turned round, waiting for them, she made a great effort and held back her tears.

They joined up again. It was already starting to get dark, sooner than they would have thought. The black bell-tower of Damme, that had seemed close because of the great clarity of the air, withdrew into the land. It was too late to think of continuing, so they turned round and retraced their steps, walking together now, and in silence, the two women a little weary from the keen wind and the walk, Wilhelmine because of the irrevocable fate that had befallen her heart, where she seemed to be cradling a stillborn child. Hans, his eyes on the darkening plain, was silently praying.

Within them and around them was the melancholy of things that are drawing to a close—the end of hope and the end of the day. Seeing Hans and Wilhelmine's air of constraint, Mevr. Cadzand suspected something sad had occurred. With a sense of foreboding and a heavy heart, she watched the sunshine die away in their eyes, for the mist was thickening, ascending, rising up from the countryside around to veil the sun, which faded behind drifts of diaphanous tulle, pallid muslin.

By the time they reached the town, twilight had fallen. The windmills along the embankments, motionless, half submerged, appeared as geometrical shapes, like crosses on graves.

The sun had disappeared, gone to who knows what winter quarters in the deepest recesses of the sky. Wilhelmine, now that it was dark, no longer attempted to hold back her tears. And Hans was still praying, thanking God for having stood by him in his trial and for sending the sign which he had seen in the final appearance of that day's sun in the mist—very pale, a paten, a host, a tonsure—as if to remind him of his vocation.

VIII

Often with very young women self-esteem is stronger than love. Wilhelmine suffered because her beautiful dream had come to an end, because she realised Hans didn't love her, never could love her. She had dreamt up a future full of such affection, she had worshipped him with such passion. Who will ever know what she said when she talked to the image of him she had inside her? With what burning looks she devoured him, without anyone noticing, every time they were together! But how was it that he had not felt those looks, which should have pierced him to the heart, leaving it scorched? And how many times did she dream of him at night! What beautiful dreams! She saw herself, alone with him, in unknown lands. She was wearing the white gown of her first ball; he kissed her and she kissed him. A divine feeling, and so strong it woke her up, astonished and sad to find herself alone in her bedroom, in the dark. The moon was shining through the tulle curtains... perhaps that was why she'd dreamt she was wearing a white gown. Oh, those sweet months when that love had taken over her entire being! Never again would she know a love like that. She certainly grieved for the end of her love; but she suffered just as much for having been scorned.

She no longer saw Hans's radiant face, which she tried to remember precisely every night in order to carry it with her into the depths of her sleep. Now, instead, she saw his cold features, calm, somewhat hard, indifferent, from that last day when she had ventured to confess her feelings. He had not shown any emotion, not even for a single moment! Had an over-rigid faith dried up his heart? Let him become a priest, then, it was best for both of them. She would have been unhappy with him.

Wilhelmine had told her mother everything, adding that from now on she didn't want to see Hans again. She resented him for having spurned her and also she would feel too embarrassed in his presence. Mevr. Daneele only visited her friend now and then, and she went alone.

The house in Blinde-Ezelstraat fell more and more silent. Hans became more stay-at-home than ever, more devout as well. He went to mass every morning, as always, but he often went back to the church in the afternoon to follow the Stations of the Cross or to light a candle. He went to confession and communion every week.

The rest of the time he remained shut up in his large room on the first floor. He had abandoned his work, the study he had started on the Bruges Beguinage; he thought it too profane. He spent all his time on his vocation, preparing for his life in religious orders. One day Mevr. Cadzand found among his papers some correspondence from the monastery of the Dominicans in Ghent, the one he had decided to enter, following the retreat where a father from that order had been the preacher. And now the Superior had sent a letter in reply to one Hans must have sent asking for information. It contained all the details relating to entry into the community, the noviciate, occupations, observances, the spiritual rule, which was the true handrail onto which the monks hold in order to climb the staircase of the Hours without falling. Looking at Hans's habits, Mevr. Cadzand realised he was already following it almost completely, living in her house the life he would live in the monastery later on. He was already half a monk—and half dead to her.

But still she was determined to persist, she would fight on to the very end. What would become of her if Hans were to leave? She would spend her life going from room to room, looking for him. She would walk round the empty house as if she were walking round a ruin. Hans! Hans! Was it for this that she had brought him into the world, pampered, cosseted, kissed him, watched over him, tucked him up in swaddling clothes which her fingers alone had sewn. Now he wanted to go away, leaving her all alone. To be alone! Is that not what people who are dying are afraid of, is that not what makes us fear the tomb?

Seeing the new, stricter way of life Hans had adopted, since he had received the information from the Superior of the Dominicans, she realised that any hope she was left with was very faint. Even the charms of her sweet accomplice, the adorable Wilhelmine, had failed. Hans's heart had not responded, would never respond.

Already he was colder, more detached in the way he behaved towards her. He still accompanied her to mass every morning, but after that she didn't see him at all for the rest of the day, apart from mealtimes. He shut himself away in his meditations, his pious books, above all the sermons of Lacordaire and other Dominicans. In that way he was preparing himself for preaching, which is the occupation and glory of that order. He wrote speeches, homilies, sometimes speaking out loud in his room, which frightened Mevr. Cadzand at first, when she went in one day and saw him standing up and gesticulating, casting words through the open window. Like St Francis of Assisi preaching the gospel to the birds and the fish, Hans was preaching to the swans on the distant canals, to the trees on the quais, to the smoke, the bells, to everything that passed, imprinted itself on the mist, occupied the silence.

Part Three

I

Hans's heart had not yielded. Now it was the turn of Hell to launch an attack on his flesh.

Mevr. Cadzand recalled having seen, some time in the past, an extraordinary picture, a Temptation of St Anthony, but not with several women offering themselves, as in those of Breughel and Teniers; in this picture it was a single woman who, completely naked, had replaced Christ on the cross, exposing her flesh on the very wood, her body forming another cross and crowned with roses. A temptation that was all the more redoubtable because it was entirely focused. In the others the hermit had the time to stop himself, to escape, because he had to choose. In this one the danger was increased because it was unified.

And one day Mevr. Cadzand realised that a similar temptation had reared its head in the solitude where Hans passed his days. He was shielded from the general danger posed by women. But the Fiend is wily, he took up residence in one woman, choosing the one that suited his purposes, the shimmering features of the eternal Eve with her insidious tongue. He came to tempt him at home, in his own house, with a constant presence he had no reason to regard with suspicion.

This Ursula was pretty and had such an innocent air, all the better to seduce him, without putting him on his guard. One morning she came to work for Mevr. Cadzand, whose chambermaid had left to get married. As a replacement? Oh, no, not really. Barbara, the old cook, was very capable and could manage the household almost on her own. At most she was taken on under the pretext of doing a little sewing, looking after the linen. In reality, however, she had come from the depths of eternity to bring Hans's misfortune. Our destiny will be fulfilled and often it employs the first messenger it finds, any accomplice to achieve its ends. In this case, however, the choice turned out to be well made. Ursula was attractive. Mevr. Cadzand herself was glad she had taken her into service. The house was transformed. Do new faces rejuvenate old houses? she asked herself. In actual fact it was Ursula's beauty, her artless smile, which brightened everything up; it was her eyes that lit up the rooms, as if two extra windows had been made.

Oh, her eyes! Truly eyes of innocence, spacious and blue, eyes like a month of Mary, like wells full of sky! But there was more than their colour to make one respond to their charm. Their shape as well, their movement, for these eyes seemed to be living a life of their own, had the air of only just having settled in her face. When Ursula looked at something, her eyes seemed to leave her lids, to approach, to come to rest, to give the warmth of a touch. Eyes that enticed, like lips. Eyes that gave kisses which landed everywhere, burning, maddening. That is what she did to Hans, the very first time she saw him, immediately stirred, captivated by his pale, handsome face, his turbulent hair.

Hans felt these big eyes fix on him over all of his skin, felt the strange, brushing caress, the tingling the inert canals must feel at night, when the star-studded sky is reflected in them.

What were these eyes, burning like stars, which had lighted on him, multiplied? When he got back to his room after the meal when he had first encountered her, he felt quite strange, as if something unusual had happened, as if he had spent too long studying the examination of conscience for the sixth and the ninth commandments in his prayer book. An indefinable but disturbing sensation. Without knowing why, the name of the young woman came back to him: Ursula, the name of Memling's virgin, while he was called Hans, like the painter. But do things not attract each other? And what we call chance, is it not simply a sign, a warning from fate?

Beneath the appearance of a Gothic virgin—the charm of the fair, blue eyes, honey-coloured hair—Ursula was of a sensual nature. At twenty, in the big cities, she had quickly slipped into love affairs. Now, in the monastic celibacy of Bruges, she was roused, tempted by Hans's youthfulness. She started to prowl round him, letting her rustling skirt shiver across his door while he was working, waiting in the corridors, on the stairs to meet him, to brush against him. Hans, without analysing things, started to feel he was under siege.

II

Until then Hans had not even looked at women. He was a complete innocent, a virgin with a double virginity, not simply of the body but of the mind as well, never having known nor wanted to penetrate the mystery of the sexes, which remained obscure to him. A mind that had not yet lost its bloom. Flesh intact, consecrated, like the virgin wax of church tapers.

At most he had had a premonition of woman on the evening when Wilhelmine had come dressed for the ball, seeing her shoulders, her chest, the details... Now the memory had returned when he had been looked at by Ursula. Beneath her severe bodice he saw her half dressed as well, pink and white...

The evil vision haunted him, especially when Ursula had magnetised him for some length of time with her calculated looks. Those eyes ever wandering, abolishing the space between her and him, settling on his face, tickling his hands, kissing his lips and appearing even to slip under his clothes, to gather nectar from his heart, to plunder, caress, burn, fondle and put their mark on his whole body.

What was it she wanted from him? What was this strange woman who had arrived at their house one morning, who seemed so little suited to her position, truly too refined, as if she were simply using it as a pretext to approach him, to fill him with this uneasy feeling, the restlessness of a garden before a storm, when the wind sets the trees billowing. He started to sense the spell she cast, without being able to avoid it. It was in vain that he had resolved not to look at Ursula any more, to make sure to turn away from the snare of her face, he was still subject, through the air, to her insistent looks. All the time Ursula's eyes were on him, he felt them sticking to his skin, alive, opening their caskets... Even away from her, when he was alone, locked away in his room, her two great eyes followed him. He was caught between them, as if between two implacable candles. What frightened him most was that they even followed him to church. When the priest, before mass, made the sign of the cross with a large monstrance, it was a huge blue eye instead of the pale host, Ursula's eye appearing captive, behind glass.

From this point on they haunted him daily, unceasingly. He saw them at night as well, her two beautiful eyes lying beside him, changing shape in every dream phantasm. All at once Hans feels her blond hair growing on the pillow, extending to the size of a field, immense, ripe and ready for harvest, with two single cornflowers in it, Ursula's eyes, hidden, lost, but which he has to find at all cost before daybreak. Then an abrupt darkness—and Ursula's eyes are signal discs at a railway station. From there they take flight, flit about... A peacock is displaying on some steps, its tail a fan of eyes, a hundred pupils like Ursula's pupils... Then the eyes fly up higher, a face forms, they are kites, they are blue moons... Suddenly they tumble back down to earth, shrivelled, cold, tiny, unmoving turquoises which, a moment later melt, flow, liquidise and turn into the sea, a Mediterranean blue where Ursula's head emerges from among the waves, attached to Wilhelmine's naked breast, finishing up as a siren.

It was with terror and aching all over that Hans emerged from these feverish nights full of visions. But by day it was even worse. How disturbing for an adolescent in whose house a young woman has come to live. Especially disturbing when the woman's desire is prowling round, cajoling him.

For Ursula had conceived a passion for Hans's proud looks, his fine hair... She became more daring, aware of the hold she was gradually exerting over him. Not content with looking with eyes that spoke to him, that kissed him, she became bolder, more decisive, making furtive physical contact.

When she had some object to give him, his post to bring, she tried to brush his hand, to feel his skin. Those first little touches of love in which two people meet, in which they already possess each other in a small way!

In the evening Hans was in the habit of asking for a carafe of freshly drawn water for the night. Ursula waited until the very last moment, only taking it up after Hans had gone to his bedroom, which was on the second floor, above his mother's; on the first floor he just had his study. Before he could close the door, Ursula, who was keeping watch, immediately came in, put down the carafe and gave Hans one of those long looks in which she seemed to come out of her eyes. Often the young man turned away, pretending to be occupied with something. Occasionally he didn't manage to take cover in time and Ursula's eyes hit him full in the face, like two flowers thrown at him. They would make him stagger. Ursula would linger, would go and turn up the lamp on the pretext that it was smoking... She would give Hans another look, a more passionate one. Now her eyes dilated—Hans's bed was reflected in them, opening out in the blue of their alcove.

Hans was trembling; his breath was taken away and his cheeks burned as a hot flush spread over them.

Finally Ursula decided to leave. But her 'Good night' was so insinuating, so slow-drawn-out with regret and mute supplication...

Alone at last, Hans would throw himself to his knees, beg the Virgin Mary to come to his aid and ask God's forgiveness, judging himself already in a state of sin for his acquiescence in playing with danger. For now he was aware of temptation. And what a wretched love affair he was sliding into!

There was no point in having rejected the virginal charm of Wilhelmine for this lust for a servant of which he was ashamed. But Ursula was not a servant-girl. Does a servant have those exquisite features, those manicured hands, that refinement of her whole bearing and those knowing stratagems of the mind which were leading his virtue astray? No. She was an emissary of Hell, come to the house under a pretext and conspiring in his downfall...

Hans was in a panic. He had to take precautions, deal with the situation, remove the temptation which might perhaps prove too strong for him. Yes, that would be best! He would ask his mother to dismiss Ursula. But under what pretext? On no account must his mother suspect what was behind it.

Hans was at his wit's end. And he already felt powerless to undertake any serious measures anyway. Get Ursula sacked? The poor girl was sure to cry. And the looks she would give him as she left! He couldn't go on living feeling those parting eyes forever on him, those moist eyes, eyes that he had drowned...

Ursula! Ursula! He fled her and he sought her. He asked God's aid to resist her but, as in the picture Mevr. Cadzand remembered, even when he knelt before the crucifix, it was a woman he saw there, her body forming a cross, exposing the flowers of her eyes, the flowers of her breasts, the flower of her sex—like the Five Holy Wounds blossoming with Love.

III

Mevr. Cadzand was not unaware of the game Ursula was playing, of her strange eyes that always turned towards Hans; but it was above all her son who had revealed it to her by his inner turmoil, the change in his manner. True, he was as assiduous in his devotions as ever, accompanying her to mass every morning, praying frequently. But he prayed in a different manner, the way shipwrecked mariners must pray. There was expectation, anxiety, struggle in the way he addressed God. Confusion too. He would prostrate himself, his head in his hands, withdraw behind the grille of his outstretched fingers as if to ward off a call, an insistent face. Mevr. Cadzand had no difficulty working out the situation, all the more so since she had noticed that Ursula was in Hans's bedroom for a short while in the evening. She slept directly underneath, on the floor below, and she could hear the sound of footsteps, the sound of voices very distinctly through the ceiling. Mevr. Cadzand was not particularly concerned about this. Hans was handsome and Ursula was young, it was quite natural she should respond. A mere flirtation, nothing more. In fact, without openly admitting it, Mevr. Cadzand was rather pleased by it. She saw Hans's devoutness as a guarantee against any accident.

But surely it was legitimate for her to hope some faint emotion would be aroused in him, something which would certainly not be passion but which would give him an awareness of women, a notion of what love was. Knowing himself looked at as he was looked at by her, it was impossible for him not to sense a thrill, the joy of feeling his blood flow more quickly, the desire to kiss... And that was enough to undermine his asceticism.

Once he was aware of women, sensed the delights they could offer, his devotion to God, to his vocation, would cool. His mother started to hope once more.

IV

One evening, when Mevr. Cadzand had her habitual migraine, she went to bed earlier than usual. She was resting, her aching head flung back among the pillows, in a daze half-way between waking and sleeping, that state in which you seem to be at the bottom of something transparent and extremely sensitive to impressions. It feels as if you are surrounded by water, as if you have fallen into a mirror, as if you have been banished to a greenhouse, where every sound is exaggerated on the glass.

Your senses become incredibly acute. Even muffled steps, a voice close to silence, are enough for your hearing to be roused, for your attention to respond, to be aware.

Mevr. Cadzand was dozing, but that did not stop her recognising Hans's footsteps on the stairs as he went up to bed at his normal time. A moment later she heard Ursula go into the room above her, doubtless taking Hans his carafe of fresh water for the night as usual. But then she heard them speaking, in very low voices. This time Ursula did not leave after a short while, to return to her own room next to old Barbara's. She was still there. Astonished, Mevr. Cadzand shook off some of her hazy sleep. She listened. The two voices were recognisable, alternating then interweaving. Hans and Ursula... yes, it was them. Speaking in faint whispers. Then one of the voices grew louder, the woman's voice, sounding urgent, impassioned. What could be happening? Mevr. Cadzand had sat up, leaning back against the pillows. The sound of steps—someone running away, one would have said, across the room. The chandelier above her bed trembled a little, shaking its hail of crystals, as if in a draught.

Then a sudden halt. One single step, slow and together, like a couple clasping each other and heading... Mevr. Cadzand got up in panic. Was she dreaming? Was Hans perhaps ill? Mevr. Cadzand was about to open the door, go out onto the landing, call out, when the two voices were heard once more. Yes, Ursula was still there. She spoke again and Hans replied—confused mumblings, murmurs of rapture, utterances starting from one set of lips and ending from the other's. The sound of kisses scorched the silence...

Mevr. Cadzand, dumbstruck, realised what was happening in the room above. How had it come about that Hans, so pure, so devout, had succumbed to temptation? But those glances Ursula had been giving him for days now! It was she who had seduced him, who at that very moment was teaching him, initiating him.

A nocturnal scene, as disturbing and moving as a play or a crime. Mevr. Cadzand was the audience, so to speak, hearing the noises, the voices, following each stage. The scene was there for her in the way objects are there for the mirror, she had to suffer it despite herself, to live it out in reflections. Everything came back to her across the years. Mevr. Cadzand was trembling, horrified. And yet she felt that a sacred Act was being performed. The introduction to love is a kind of ordination. True, it was not the union acceptable in the eyes of God she had dreamt of for him in Wilhelmine's arms. But the flesh has its own secrets. At first Mevr. Cadzand had been shocked, scandalised, but who knows, perhaps passion is right and all the things we call debasing, demeaning, a misalliance are nothing but prejudices imposed by class, education, ancestry? Nature creates couples without worrying about their backgrounds. It is not we who choose—it is destiny that brings us together, ties and unties the knot. Does not the wind mingle the reeds by the river banks and make them kiss each other at random? All creatures are the same in the nakedness of love as they are in the nakedness of death. Love, as well as death, makes all men equal.

Thinking about it, Mevr. Cadzand felt that at least for Hans it was a young woman—and a beautiful one at that—who was revealing the great mystery to him. Ursula desired him, loved him, there was no question of money passing between them, as there was for so many other men. His first night of love would, after all, have something nuptial about it.

Mevr. Cadzand listened, her emotions in ferment. She recalled other nights, the ones when Hans was conceived among similar kisses, her widow's flesh burnt with the memory, the echo of long-ago sensual pleasure... Yes, Hans was a love child. How could it be that he had escaped the desire for the sacred spasm? Her head was on fire with a thousand thoughts jostling, overriding each other and one emerged, returned, revived her: perhaps this would be her salvation and happiness. How could Hans persist in his vocation after the revelation of what a woman had to offer? Would he dare to commit himself to the vow of chastity now that he had known sin and the delight of the flesh? Mevr. Cadzand was carried away by immense hope. No! She would not dismiss Ursula in the morning, she would close her eyes, for the moment. And she would not reproach her son, she would let him become accustomed to love, to sensual pleasure since it was the only way to stop him taking orders, to keep him for herself. Chance had seen to everything. She should not go against chance, it knew better than she did. For it had been naïve of her to imagine that Wilhelmine and the cool lily of her love would be enough. Ursula was the rose in full bloom, the flower of sensuality, the scent of which is intoxicating, as if one were dying a little of too much ecstasy! She will have given him a taste for life, a taste for life's garden, now that he knows the rose in full bloom, the secret rose of the flesh!

V

When Mevr. Cadzand came down next morning she was greatly concerned. Ursula was busy tidying up in the dining room, calm and smiling, her cheeks just a little more pink than usual, her steps just a little more languid, as if weighed down with a weight of happiness. She exuded a sense of joy and her blond hair had a quiver of triumphant brass. Especially when Hans came down, pale as usual but with his turbulent locks creased in a way that was not usual. Mevr. Cadzand watched them closely. Surreptitiously Ursula sent him victorious glances, assailed him with her predator's eyes. And Hans, sitting at the table for his breakfast, twisted and turned, appearing constrained, appearing to defend himself against something invisible that kept piercing his guard. It was Ursula's eyes, whose mysterious power was already coursing along his nerves, both burning and caressing. Her eyes would go to his face then move away, just as spiders leave their web on a thread attached to it which they know will take them back again. And, truly, Ursula's darting eyes were blue spiders on Hans's skin, slipping everywhere, titillating him with a thousand invisible tiny feet, caressing, irritating, tickling him with a multitude of little, infinitesimal spasms, a thousand sparks reigniting in the cold ashes of pleasure. For he was still afire from the night, he could not stop thinking of the Act: disgust and delight! So that was the great mystery, the Eternal Love for which men exerted, exiled, ruined themselves, suffered and killed!

Hans Cadzand's Vocation

Fleeting ecstasy, a shuddering, writhing as if, for a moment, a bolt of lightning were passing through us which would inoculate us with heaven; and then also a fainting, sinking, as if, for a moment, we were being engulfed in a sea of wines and perfumes! Hans recalled it, analysed it, but, what was curious, in thinking about the Act, he hardly thought of the woman at all. Ursula herself had seemed to remain so alien to him... They had not been truly joined except in that. Doubtless it had been because all she had done had been to carry out the implacable destiny, the secret mission of the Fiend. Now, looking at it honestly, in the clear light of day, he saw that clearly. She had come the previous evening, taking advantage of the darkness, that poor counsellor, to give him the fruit of sin. The eternal Eve! Perhaps she wasn't even to blame, perhaps she had been tempted and lured herself. Hans bore her no grudge. It was the Fiend made flesh in her, talking with her lips, putting a fire into her kisses which could only be that of Hell.

How could he have yielded, he, the chosen one of God, rich in grace, he who had been called, as he used to say with pride, thinking of his vocation?

Hans was overcome with remorse. At mass, which he attended with his mother, he did not dare turn towards the altar, nor towards the host at the moment of the Elevation. It seemed to him that if he looked at it he would see the face of Jesus, covered in tears and blood because of his betrayal. He prayed; he asked forgiveness; but at every moment Ursula interposed herself between God and him. Her eyes were always there, fluttering round him, magnetised; then they landed on his skin, merged with his flesh.

At lunch Ursula, who was serving at table, brushed against him, caressed him with her dress. Back up in his first-floor room, where he worked, his obsession increased. At moments an after-shudder went through his bones, the silent exhalation which still tinges the sky with sulphur, even though the storm is past. More sinful curiosity mingled with it. He had seen Wilhelmine's shoulders, her throat displayed, that suggestion of bold, pink nudity... He thought of Ursula, still veiled for him... as evening approached temptation returned like a fever approaching its crisis...

And thus it continued for several days. Hans relapsed into sin. He came to know the whole mystery. Ursula, who now stayed in his room until late into the night, alluring and obliging, revealed the intimate parts of her flesh, the warm valley, the pair nestling there, everything he could hardly make out in Wilhelmine's tulle bodice. The marvel of breasts! The frenzy of young hands fingering them as if they were about to gather them, those bunches of white grapes crowned with a blue grape, to press from them an elixir of joy against all sorrow. The beauty of breasts! Their rhythm, their ebb and flow like that of the sea... And above all their softness, a pillow of oblivion, the fullness of down, the scent of lavender, a place to sleep, perhaps even to die! How can one free oneself from them, renounce them, whose mere absence leaves our hands impoverished, as if bereft?

However, amid these sensual images assailing him, Hans maintained the faithful presence of the Virgin Mary inside himself and called on her for help. Does one not often see in the ancient towns of Flanders, even in the run-down quarters of debauchery, a Madonna in a glass cabinet, a stone niche? And flowers filling the air with fragrance, candles burning...

Hans had not betrayed his former devotion, nor despaired. As the end of the week approached he even seemed to pull himself together. His revulsion at his sin took on clearer contours: yes, he was in a state of mortal sin and, if he were to die suddenly, as can happen, he was bound to be damned. His fear of Hell returned, all the imaginings, the terrifying pictures of the college sermons. He was also overcome with sincere sorrow; he had caused God distress; he had made the Five Wounds and the Sacred Heart of Jesus bleed again. At the moment he was unworthy and despicable, he had strayed from the path of his vocation.

One day Mevr. Cadzand, who was observing him closely, found him completely wretched. It was as if he had suffered a great calamity, he was no longer pale, but white. He sat down at the table but ate almost nothing and didn't speak. His eyes were reddened, as if he had been crying. Now he kept well out of the way of Ursula's eyes, as one does of fearsome animals one is afraid of. As he sat down, he had carefully said grace and, above all, made the sign of the cross, very deliberately and emphatically, as if to envelop himself in it, to carry out an exorcism.

His mother understood the struggle that was going on inside him and was delighted that his piety was already winning, and so quickly. That meant he would not fall prey to depravity, but he would have been sufficiently acquainted with passion to know the ecstasy it can bring and would not now dare devote his life to a celibacy with no way out.

This was what his mother was counting on, hoping that this truly providential event would turn out for the best: Hans would definitely be cured of his desire to take holy orders with their harsh law of chastity; on the other hand, it was clear to see that he was pulling himself together, was regaining control of himself... But at the cost of what despair! As if, emerging from a storm, he were aghast at how his soul had been laid waste. Expressions of fear, sadness, horror, dismay, confusion passed across his face one after another or at the same time. He seemed to be threatened, tormented, haunted, suffering in his conscience and in his body all at once.

Mevr. Cadzand was alarmed. 'Are you ill?'

At once he stood up and left the room, as if she had touched a wound and he had to run to a spring to soothe it. He spent hours by himself, locked in his room. Mevr. Cadzand, keeping a watch for him, heard him walking up and down, talking out loud but no longer practising sermons, as he had done when he was reading Lacordaire and the preachers; there was nothing oratorical about it now, but a level voice, infinitely sad, the sound of a lament, doubtless a prayer, a sick prayer crouched on the ground and trying to get up. It had something of the murmurings of processions of pilgrims on the highroads.

Suddenly his door creaked, his steps echoed on the stairs. A moment later, contrary to all his habits and despite the rain lashing the windows, she heard him go out, without a word to anyone, as if to avoid having to say goodbye, having his resolve weaken in a farewell.

Mevr. Cadzand was alarmed at this unaccustomed departure. She had already seen him at lunchtime, so disturbed, so strange! And that groan in the afternoon, which was still echoing round the corridor like the lingering vibration of a bell...

What had happened? What was going to happen? She knew that Hans was impressionable, highly strung, sometimes prone to sudden decisions. What if his despair at his fall had left him distraught? What if his fear of Ursula, whom he felt too weak to oppose, had caused him to flee? Perhaps he was going to leave, to seek immediate refuge with the Dominicans of Ghent, where it appeared he already had a place reserved? But that would mean that the religious vocation, that she feared so much and that she thought had been permanently ousted by passion, was going to be fulfilled immediately? What unhappiness for her hopes to be dashed just when she imagined them safe at last!

She was seized with panic. Hans! Hans! Where was her son, who had left looking distraught, gone out without reason or purpose, what goal was he heading for as he made his way across the town, where the rain was getting heavier, weeping on the roofs, speckling the flat water of the canals? Overcome with anxiety and fearing some calamity, Mevr. Cadzand could stand it no longer. She threw on a coat over her tea-gown, hurriedly pinned on a hat and, despite the dreadful weather, rushed out as if she had to save her child and every minute counted.

She wandered hither and thither, passing along the canals without daring to look at the water, nor at the dark tunnels under the old bridges, wondering if Hans, in his distress, had decided to drown his despair in it. Then another fear came to haunt her. Perhaps he had decided to leave, to flee the sin and temptation of his home? Immediately she turned off and headed for the station. Hans was not there and during that time no train had left in the direction she feared. Back in the street, Mevr. Cadzand started wandering round again; the rain persisted, soaking her, discolouring the pavement, gathering between the paving stones like fonts full of tears.

A terrible feeling, in the rain, to find oneself wandering, in flight, one's existence in ruins! To be no more than a soiled leaf from the tree of life, to curl up, a prey to autumn, blown along towards death!

Mevr. Cadzand kept walking, mechanically now, with the impression she had walked to the end of the day and to the end of the world. And thoughts were flying round and round inside her head. What had happened was her fault: she had defied God by trying to keep her son from Him, she was truly selfish and only thought of herself. A mother who dreams of keeping her son with her was asking too much. But above all she was to blame for the recent events: in order to achieve her goal, that is to tear him away from his vocation in the Church, she had tolerated Ursula's little game. To be frank, she had almost desired and instigated it. Otherwise she would not have employed her, so pretty—too pretty, with those eyes full of intoxicating promise. True, she had considered the danger when she had taken her on, but basically she had just smiled, content with the way chance had arranged things. She had connived at it. It was a grave sin in a mother and now God was punishing her... Hans! Hans! Where was her son? Had she lost her son?

With these thoughts going round and round in her head, she had continued, in the rain, to wander, to meander hither and thither through the maze of the streets of Bruges, the winding alleyways, the silent crossroads. After many twists and turns she found herself, without knowing how she came there, outside the Church of Our Lady. Crows were garlanding the old tower like a flight of lost souls. A bell rang out, inexorably. Every toll fell from the top of the tower, fell into her soul like a stone into a pool, making ripples in her soul, circles of sadness spreading—and of remorse as well.

The church door was not closed. She went in... almost no one in the nave, a few women of the common people praying, in the attitude particular to Flemish piety: arms raised, held out in a cross, unmoving. With their long black mantles they looked like crucified bells.

Everything was frozen, dead, dark. A few lamps cast their light, wrought brass encasing a night-light of red glass. It was like blood burning and it gave the side chapels a cryptlike terror. A vast silence prickled by the raindrops on the stained-glass windows. And a smell of stale incense, of soiled altar cloths, of candles—dead from bewailing themselves—tainted the air, turned one's stomach.

All at once Mevr. Cadzand heard a noise, the creak of woodwork. Was it one of the choir stalls where some canon had been praying, indistinguishable from the shadow? Or a confessional where the unsuspected penitent was getting up? Indeed, a moment later Mevr. Cadzand saw the figure of a man emerge, darker than the gloom around, approach, kneel down. She almost cried out. She had recognised Hans. Yes! Hans was there! He hadn't gone away. And the canals... Oh, no, no, the sole inhabitants of the canals were the swans. Hans was alive, Hans was there, close to her. He had been to confession, that was all. He was praying.

His mother was delirious, out of her mind, she could have shouted for joy in the church. She had to force herself not to call out to her son, her son who was found, saved... Hans! Hans!

Now the mystery was cleared up. For the last couple of days she had seen that Hans was regaining control of himself, liberating himself. It was the paleness of the struggle that was over that marked his face now. When he left the house abruptly, it was because he already felt himself victorious. And his sin only lay heavy on him because he had killed it inside himself...

Now he was on his knees, down there, in front of her, doubtless reciting the penitence imposed on him, but pardoned, purified, his calm regained.

His mother waited. When, after a long time, he made the sign of the cross and headed for the door, she left her seat, followed him, accosted him by the stoup.

'What, is that you?' Hans said.

'Yes. I came to pray as well.'

They left, silent, in the persistent rain, which was now turning to vapour, a fine drizzle, water dust. Hans felt his heart melt with sweetness, the melancholy joy of convalescence, which always seems slightly laden with concern about the future course of the illness of which one thought one was going to die... After a long silence Hans said—it cost him an effort but he was determined to make a request which he knew was questionable but necessary—'Don't you think we ought to dismiss Ursula? She's not a Christian, she's not the right kind of person for us.'

His mother understood the internal struggle that had reached its conclusion, his firm resolve not to fall into sin again, the promise to his father confessor. She agreed immediately and said, to set his mind at rest, 'Yes, Hans, she'll leave tomorrow.'

Night had already fallen when they returned to the old house in Blinde-Ezelstraat. And when, a little later, Hans retired to his room on the second floor, Mevr. Cadzand, who was keeping watch, heard him turn the key in the door at once.

It was the end of the kisses, the madness, the supreme Act, and silence flowed into the stairs, the corridor, that silence which follows all short celebrations, the pained silence of public parks when the music has ceased, the crowd departed and darkness descends.

Epilogue

The years have passed, Hans is now close to thirty. He still lives with his mother and he has never spoken to her of his vocation again. He is still as pious, as ardent in prayer, as assiduous in attending mass, but he has deemed himself irrevocably lost for Divine Election. True, others who had sinned and repented still entered the white cloisters, the fresh courtyards, the closed cells where the Spirit resides. The scruples which halted him on the threshold seem excessive to those who know nothing of what there had been between God and him. God had chosen him for a high purpose alone and he had proved unworthy of that purpose. God had called him to be a shining light of holiness, a vessel of chastity. The vessel had been cracked by sin and, however well it seemed covered over, something would always filter through. But what if that something should be the very blood of Christ entrusted to it? And if the precious blood were seen to come out in tiny drops, a red condensation perpetuating round the cracked vessel the sweat of the agony in the garden on the Mount of Olives? Nothing could make the vessel intact again. Nothing could stop what happened from having happened. It was beyond remedy. God no longer wanted him, no longer sought him, since he had become a different person.

So Mevr. Cadzand kept her son and will definitely keep him until the end of her life, for henceforward no woman, no love will be able to take him away from her. He emerged from his first sin of the flesh as if from an abyss that was not to be approached again. But despite having kept him, as she so strongly desired, she is unhappy, full of regret, feels at fault for having dared to try and wrest her son from God. She could not overcome God. And today she is more distresed at her apparent victory that she would have been from a defeat. She realises that she has ruined Hans's life, and even her own. It would have been better to know that her son was happy far away from her than to see him unhappy close to her.

Hans is inconsolable at having failed in his vocation. He has cloistered himself in the old house in Blinde-Ezelstraat, where the life he lives is less that of a layman than of an ecclesiastic; he lives away from the world, like a solitary ascetic, detached from everything and only going out once a day to accompany his mother to eight-o'clock mass.

Thus it was that they were seen passing every morning at the same time (envied by other mothers who had no idea of their situation), as the morning mist cleared, along the old quais, at a funereal pace, and so shut off from everything outside their own selves that even the swans on the canals, sensitive as they are, did not take fright, did not feel the shadow of the couple in black stain their white silence with mourning.

At School

Every year when October returns I recall, almost with terror, the moment when, at the end of the holidays, I would go back to school. A dismal season which, from the depths of the years regards me with the white eyes of a statue on a tomb. Those who went to school in Paris know nothing of this sorrow. Here at least something of the noise of the big city comes in through the doors and windows, something of its pleasures, its music, of its vices too, intoxicating adolescent curiosity—in short something to give you a desire for life.

But out in the provinces the great colleges run by the Church are so gloomy and so grey! Mine was as enclosed as a seminary. And, all around, the dead town grieved in the tear-ridden concert of its bells. There was a central courtyard, a strip of ground as bare as a beach where the ebbing tide has left its sadness. Not even a few trees to liven it up. Alone in its gable was the implacable face of a great clock with hands that came together, parted; the hours, as they were struck, fell on us so plaintively it made them seem dark. It was like a rain of iron and ash. A dreary, invariable existence behind the high walls of the yard blocking out the sun. It was there that my soul fell out of love with life for having learnt too much of death!

Death! It was death that the priests, who were our masters, placed among us from the moment we got back. We came from our homes with our pretty outfits of fresh, new linen.

They added the funeral pall, its black velvet with yellow braid. All we wanted to do was to grow up, to learn so that we could finally walk alone, love, conquer the world, live! They taught us to prepare for a good death.

And everything had a taste of death, as if by design, even the walks the boarders took one afternoon every week. We left in a long file, three by three, going at a swift pace through the centre of the town, along the canals with their lifeless water, across the deserted districts round the Cathedral close, to get as quickly as possible to the dismal suburbs where the cemeteries are. Almost every time we encountered a hearse, a large, draped carriage with undertakers wearing black, sinister three-cornered hats. As soon as they left the centre of the town, the horses were set at a trot and the carriage sped along, swaying on the uneven cobbles. How frightening for the poor deceased who might be hurt by the severe jolts! Whichever direction our band of children took, to all parts of the town, we always ended up at cemeteries, which are so desolate in that austere province which had never acquired the art of decorating tombs: none of those bright flowers, those ribbons, all the funerary knick-knacks, those white pearls that look like tears gathered in a bouquet. Nothing but the black tresses of the willows, the geometrical firs, an arrangement betokening inevitability and abandonment.

I had the feeling that we ourselves were being led as a flock to death; the vague feeling a lamb marked with a red cross might have as it is being led to the abattoir. And we went, hurried all the way along the evening road by a tall, bony priest, black as a shepherd's dog. That is how they spoilt our joy in nature for good. Running water, the wind shaking itself in the corn, birds, wide-open spaces, the sight of the whole sky, the elegant lines of animals, trees with the foliage making a noise like a crowd, nothing delights me, nothing intoxicates me with being alive. All I can see in the countryside is our final resting place.

Death! Even more than on those melancholy walks, we felt it around us during the religious services. Especially at the time of the annual retreat, which took place a few days after school began again in October, as if they could not wait before once more confronting our childhood with Eternity, the only thing that matters.

Generally the retreat was preached by an outside preacher and consisted of four days of sermons, meditations and pious exercises, concluding with general confession and the Eucharist. From the pulpit the priest held forth with gloomy vehemence about the shortness of life, the inevitability of death, the horror of sin; then, after some cautious circumlocution, which some of us understood clearly while others, who had remained more chaste, found rather baffling, he went on to talk about the Sixth and Ninth Commandments. It is above all the traditional sermon on Hell that has remained a cruel memory; every year the preacher dealt with that terrifying subject in the evening, when the church was already submerged in darkness. He painted a tragic picture in red: an abyss suddenly opening up, the eternal inferno, bodies clothed in fire, arms tattooed with burns, lips pleading for a drop of water, a tear from God to refresh them—which will never come. Darkness reigned. Just a few candles were lit with flames which stretched out and shifted in the draught. We were terrified. The red of Hell was around us already. The preacher's voice could be heard, but he himself had retreated into the gloom, was part of the gloom. It was as if the mouth of darkness had spoken. And it addressed us in the tones of an inquisitor. Each one of us seemed to be marked out, threatened. It said, 'There is your fate, if you die. You will be clothed in fire. And there are cases of sudden death at all ages.'

And already we were trembling, as if with a shiver of the death throes...

Since we were young, we did not feel very threatened despite these constant reminders of death. However there were often boys who were ill among us. They were taken to the sick-bay, the room whose windows had white cotton curtains, two windows, the last of the tall building running along the courtyard. The sick-bay! What a sad sound the word had! We saw it as the antechamber of eternity. Every time one of us had fallen ill and was confined to bed, we looked at the two high windows in fear and trembling. There was almost always some pale pupil to be seen, with migraine, toothache, wearing a white bandage round his cheeks or forehead. How melancholy it was to see from afar, from down in the yard, young faces with those headbands of rime, those bandages of snow. It was as if war had passed through, you felt they were little wounded soldiers and there was blood under the gauze.

During those dark years there was a suddenly a bright spot, a marvellous clearing, a heavenly moon rising from among the dark poplars. They wanted to introduce us to death—our adolescence introduced itself to love. How did the revelation take place? Through a book. I will never forget the indescribable enchantment. The college library was strict, carefully sifted, pruned, puritan, irreproachable. Nothing but the lives of saints, historical works, accounts of voyages. There was also among them, by what chance I could not say, *Harmonies poétiques et religieuses*. We only had half an hour for reading, in the evening, after prep. As if by magic there was an apparition

At School

in the course of the mysterious book, which started to sing between my fingers like a piece of music—Lamartine! His face materialised on the white of the pages, handsome as a god... and another face emerged beside it: Elvire! Their hair intermingled... The Mediterranean drew them to its shore... The lines murmuring one after another. They were blue waves... and they broke. I too was walking there, kissed by those waves... Where was I? I was being carried off on a dream journey... The big lamps in the study room shed a radiance pale as moonlight... Their heavy shades seemed like haloes. Elvire! So she was love! Oh, her face, her hair black as night; her olive complexion, the colour of a pineapple, like that of girls from the south; and the scent of her skin which must sweeten her lips as well! Lamartine knew—since he had kissed her.

So that was love? And what else? Indescribable inner turmoil... Why did they talk to us about death, those dismal priests? There is love first. Oh, when will it come for us? Elvire was approaching. We were thinking of kisses... We were also thinking, trembling a little, of the mystery of breasts, a mystery dimly known, dimly seen on statues, glimpsed on our walks in the bared bosom of wet-nurses. An exciting vision! Our hearts seemed to stop beating. We were out of breath, as if after a race or a sudden shock. Elvire's breasts? Had Lamartine touched them, put his hands on them—his lips, as we did with our flasks in summer? Elvire! We compared her to girls we caught sight of on holiday, a cousin who had come to visit our parents with her family and whom we looked at, blushing. She was pink. Elvire was bronzed. But she, too, had a rounded bust we didn't dare look at—doubtless the same breasts as Elvire...

Oh, this first revelation of love! The touch of fever that brought a flush to our cheeks... We were no longer aware of time or place... We dreamt... We drifted... We evoked images that were full of passion but not shameless, for the moment it was solely our imagination at play. We were still innocent, sufficiently so to be quickly alarmed at these mirages, at love, at Elvire, at the cousin who resembled her. Religious fear quickly raised its head, fear of sin, the sin of bad thoughts and bad desires, into which we had perhaps slipped, the deadly sin... And the thought of death returned, the fear of death, which quickly made love flee!

Because death more than love—a too distant dream—was a reality. Especially when one of our classmates fell seriously ill. He had to go home to his parents. A few weeks later we were told he was dead. Immediately each one of us thought of the words of the preacher at the retreat. 'People die at all ages. Beware of being damned. You will be clothed in fire in Hell.' Had our poor classmate been saved? Or was he already clothed in fire? So he would have met Elvire, who was also dead... Was she damned or saved? Their memories merged... Was it him or her who was missing from that unoccupied seat in the classroom? No one would agree to sit in it. Oh, the void that we found unbearable!

It was as if an opening had been cut in a hedge in blossom to let a coffin through. A gaping hole. Were they not going to fill in the grave? His absence had to be covered over. Everyone was trembling. No one wanted to replace our dead classmate, so he seemed to keep his place, to remain with us...

A sinister emblem! Death was ever present amid our adolescence. Oh, those years when we ought to have been taught to love life but during which their sole concern was to familiarise us with death. A too-religious school. And, all around, a too-dead town! Given our fear of death, everything was transposed, took on a funereal sense, even love which approached us with the look of the dead Elvire...

To such an extent that even when the great bell rang out, when its immense sounds fell, it seemed to us, poor children that we were, that it was to fill in the silence—like the spadefuls of earth filling a grave.

The Urban Hunter

The other day I recognised my friend X from behind, walking in front of me down the avenue. You could see he was happy from his jaunty gait and from the lively flourishes of his cane with which he was drawing arabesques in the air, perhaps matching the lines on his hand containing his destiny... After a while I realised he was following a woman. What, him? A discriminating and serious man, intelligent and sociable, still attractive, who would have had no trouble making conquests in the salons of the city.

He had never been known to have an affair, nor even to flirt with women. He was married and people assumed he was quite simply faithful. But, I told myself, he showed an interest in women he saw passing in the street, so he must be a more complicated case than people assumed. However, given his discerning character it was difficult to imagine him addicted to low vice, to random lechery. He halted at the end of the avenue, as if he were giving up, and suddenly turned round in my direction. We met more or less face to face.

'Aha, I've caught you,' I said. 'You follow women.'

'Of course. That's the only reason I go out.'

My expression must have shown some surprise or a suspicion that he was being ironic, for he repeated his statement, as if his explanation was perfectly reasonable and, that being the case, it was necessary to put it into words.

'Yes,' he went on, 'everyone's away hunting during this

season. I'm not a huntsman, this is where I hunt. The great capital cities are forests teeming with game of every shape and size—women. I go out hunting every afternoon. I check the state of my gloves, my hat, my whole appearance, just as a huntsman does with his gun and his dogs. And I have the thrill, the delightful anguish of the wait, the watch, the pursuit, the kill— just like the huntsman. And there is the same variety as there is in game: there are women who flit about the street, quivering like birds, some who walk past in the brightly coloured plumage of a pheasant, others who appear and disappear among the crowd like a hare in the grass or those who would charge furiously like a boar at the first approach. Oh, to hunt all this game, to follow all these women! And, like a good huntsman, to load your gun immediately, change the ammunition, choose the right cartridge, adjust your aim. Bird-shot or buck-shot, riddle with pellets or drop with a single bullet. Accost her with a clever remark or quickly pepper her with several brief comments to benumb the protesting voice like winging a bird. That means it requires great calmness and clarity of vision to recognise immediately the type of woman, just as the huntsman can recognise the nature of the game from the noise it makes in the silence as it passes, while still invisible.'

'And there was I thinking you were a faithful husband!' I exclaimed, amused and somewhat astounded.

'But I am,' my friend replied, 'and in a very physical sense. This is a different matter. A true huntsman never eats the game he kills. He doesn't like game, neither partridge nor pheasant, nor hare, nor venison. I never sleep with the women I follow—or hunt, if you like. Hunting is a pleasure that's all in the mind, a thrill in the nerves that is sufficient unto itself. All the pleasure is in what precedes it and what follows: getting up, equipping yourself, setting off, lying in wait, tracking down your quarry, forcing it to break cover, bringing it to bay; and then all the little incidentals: the tactics, the wait, the thrill, the uncertainty of the outcome, the brief moment your quarry comes within range, on which everything depends; then afterwards: satisfied pride, the exaggerated account, to others, of your exploits... Those are the secret joys of the hunt, no matter whether the quarry is a woman or game. The moment of the shot is nothing...'

'Very witty,' I told him, 'but it seems to me to be nothing more than wit, an ingenious fantasy.'

'It's a reality. I do what I told you, I'd die of boredom just walking round the streets on my own if I hadn't invented this sport. I do hunt. There's all sorts of hunting stories I could tell! And the misadventures, the hazards of pursuit, the thrill of the little danger when you hunt the game down to its den! That's happened to me more than once. Pursuing a woman can arouse you to a fever, you can't stop... In such cases I entered the buildings where the women I was following perhaps lived, or hotels where I didn't know whether they were staying as guests or whether, as willing accomplices, they were leading me. You need a flexible mind, subtle intuition, to be able to make immediate judgments and to act on them: follow now from a distance, now from close to, hurry up or slow down, smile or put on a languorous expression, adopt a sentimental or masterful air, pursue them onto the stairs or stand outside their windows. Some women are best approached in out-of-the-way streets, others in the throng on the boulevards, some should be led into an alleyway, others to a cab. That is the way I have been proceeding, with subtle variations—a thousand subterfuges. And that up to the point at which I was certain, up to the moment when the woman acquiesced: instant docility, agreement to a rendezvous or simply amiable high spirits, still a portent of ultimate success, each was enough to satisfy me. Immediately I gave up the game. That is, I slipped away from our conversation, did not keep the promise to see her again, avoided the consummation, whichever was the case and which, after all, are but the three stages of success. It was the guarantee that mattered to me, I was happy with that once it had been given. As I said before, a true huntsman does not eat the game he kills, nor am I interested in the women I have hunted down...'

My friend fell silent. He was looking into the distance, his grey eyes already fixed on something, as if a new prey had appeared. After what he had told me, I noticed for the first time how grey his clear eyes were, a steely grey, the grey of a gun barrel... At the same time his nostrils twitched, like a hunting dog scenting a trail. It seemed to me that what he had said was true, concentrated within him was the whole apparatus of the hunt. In the distance women were walking past with their bird-like charm, their dresses as he had described them, like the brightly coloured plumage of the pheasant—game there for the hunting!

However, I had found my friend's story disturbing and was worried about him. What was this arousal with no goal, this mental debauchery? Concealing my unfavourable impression behind a smile, I still managed to express a little of my concern.

'Be careful,' I told him, 'it's a pleasure that could become dangerous. It's a strange obsession, with a touch of sadism about it, perhaps.'

'Well,' he replied, 'I'm not the only one. The great capital cities are full of hunters like me. Sometimes, when I've been following a woman for a while, I realise that there are three or four of us walking behind or alongside her. It's like a battue, a hunt where the prey are driven between several guns. Anyway, there are all sorts of hunts and widely differing tastes. And there are those who specialise. Some only like a certain type of woman, brunettes or blondes, slim ones, as slender as a sapling, or fat ones like a well-fleshed animal, there are those who only follow redheads, others young women who already have white hair. Women in mourning have their connoisseurs, in public parks where their black crepe goes well with the dead leaves. Some are only after widows—they are hunters who like to finish off game that has already be wounded. For here, too, there are different kinds of hunters. One who pursues young virgins corresponds to the huntsman who only enjoys hunting wild duck, one who persists in following severe beauties to a boar hunter.'

'And how many actually get taken?' I asked. 'If there are so many hunters in the forests of the big cities, the weak female game must often succumb.'

'Yes! They've done some statistics: among women who are accosted, one in four yields. A large proportion of those are women from the provinces and foreigners whose heads are turned by the fever of Paris: in a whirl and blind to everything around them, they easily fall. For the rest it depends on some trifle—a word, a moment, destiny, the man's technique. It's in that above all that the analogy with the huntsman is convincing. It's the same with women as with game, you miss them as often as you get them.'

A Woman in the Jardin du Luxembourg

Crossing the Jardin du Luxembourg one day, Dronsart paused for a moment, carried away by the October splendour, by the old trees adorning the horizon with russet tapestries, by the sky above with palaces crumbling in a blaze of glory, glass staircases, a vast expanse of pink embers. Evening was approaching in crimson and grey, as majestic as the end of a reign. Dronsart felt himself succumbing to the nostalgia of autumn and of the gardens. He stopped by the basin into which the jet of water fell back incessantly—unstilled desire.

His mind, over-stimulated, formed other analogies. The colour of the leaves crackling under his feet evoked that of horns sounding in forests with red foliage. And because of the contrast of colours, his attention was all the more attracted by the woman in black amid the red-and-gold fresco of the old gardens which continued inside his head. Sober and sombre dress, without her being in mourning however.

It looked as if she had taken great care to cut out any bright colours. No gay ribbons, no jewellery. Not even a flower on her hat. It seemed impossible that it had not been done deliberately, so as to be dressed in accord with her thoughts. For she looked pensive, pale in the dark cloth, like a statue representing half-mourning beside a path. She was sitting on one of the stone benches, staring into the distance, at the trees, the sunset, even farther, somewhere beyond life... Dronsart immediately felt attracted, carried away by her weary air.

Was her sadness due to some real sorrow, or was it just the bereavement of the moment?

There are nerves that feel pity, sensitive threads on which are strung all the tears of things... Dronsart had fixed a bold, but still tender gaze on the young woman. She turned her head away. He persisted, walked round the bench, finally made up his mind and went to sit down beside her. Seen from close to she was even more moving. The sky, the glass staircases, the pink embers were in her big eyes. Her mouth was a sinuous line, as if moulded from a fruit. Her shapely ear had the complex whorls of a seashell. Her copper hair epitomised the golden splendour of the autumnal gardens. And freckles here and there on her cheeks, the first dead leaves in flight... Very pale, with a delicate, white complexion which looked as if it were lit from within, like a candle burning inside a nightlight.

Dronsart, aroused, looked at her, surveying her slim hands with their criss-crossing veins, her slender waist with, rising above it, the swell of a bosom that was never at rest. It rose and fell like the water-spout before them, just as restless... Dronsart made contact with her eyes, held them, insistent. The eyes of the unknown woman acquiesced. For eyes can speak, can make themselves understood like lips. So Dronsart, pardoned in advance, was emboldened to speak to her. A tentative venture. Stammering. Words drawn out. Lips following behind when two hearts, linked by destiny, have already met and recognised each other! Dronsart spoke of the beautiful evening, of her big eyes, the loneliness of youth...

'You feel sad as well?' he asked the young woman.

'Yes!'

'Where are you going on this fine evening?'

'Nowhere.'

'You have no lover?'

'Oh, don't talk to me about love! Don't even mention the word.' She looked distraught.

'So you're going home to your parents, then?'

'Please, don't keep asking me these questions,' she begged, looking even sadder.

Her eyes misted over, her unresting bosom heaved even faster. 'I'm not going home anywhere,' she went on. 'I don't know anyone any more. We can spend the evening together if you like. But no questions. You will talk, you will say nice, sad things, very gently. And you will not ask me anything about myself.'

'Your name, just your name. I'd like to call you by your first name, so I need to know that. It's strange! It feels as if we'd known each other for ages, for months and months.'

'My name! I haven't got one any more. I'd like to have a new name for you, a different name, one just for us, just between you and me. You give me a name, as if I had just been born.'

She paused for a moment, then corrected herself sadly, 'As if I were being born again.'

At that moment two girls passed by, hitting a shuttlecock to each other as they walked along the avenue. One called out to the other, 'Nel! Nel!'

'Now that's a pretty name,' the unknown woman said. 'Nel, presumably short for Nelly. I don't know... Why not? You can call me Nel.'

Two years had passed since the first evening when Dronsart had taken the unknown woman, unresisting, to his small apartment. She had immediately felt at home, settled in, found a niche for herself.

The two years had slipped by. Dronsart still called her Nel.

They often reminded each other of the twilight of the evening when they had first met, the splendid golden trees and the fountain rising and falling like her bosom—and the pretty name tossed towards them by the little girls, like a shuttlecock, with the rackets. Nel no longer looked sad. She smiled, laughed, though always with a touch of seriousness. She seemed happy. Dronsart was happy as well. Sometimes he asked himself how this affair, which had started as the whim of an evening and was already a long liaison, was going to end. No matter! At the moment he did not feel he had the strength to break the tie that had become dear to him; above all he lacked the strength to send this woman back into the world after she had left it like someone coming out of the sea—that first evening in the Jardin du Luxembourg she had certainly seemed like someone shipwrecked on the shores of life. But what shipwrecks had she suffered? During the two years he had been living with her, he had known nothing, learnt nothing, guessed nothing. Nel had remained impenetrable. When he did venture to ask her about her past again, she would implore him, 'No! Please leave me alone!'

She seemed anxious, as if someone wanted to reopen a wound that no longer hurt. Dronsart knew nothing about her, not even her real name.

'I'm your Nel,' she would say, caressing him tenderly. 'I have a name just for our love. You should be glad I'm not the same for you as for others. Anyway, there's nothing apart from us, you're the whole world for me.'

Nel would wrap her arms round him, trembling, loving, passionate. That was the way Dronsart had found her on that very first evening, responsive to the sensual thrill, neither too experienced, nor too naïve, quickly falling into a mute abandon which said nothing about her initiation.

121

A Woman in the Jardin du Luxembourg

The mystery surrounding her remained intact. Never for one moment did she break the strict silence in which she seemed to have forgotten herself. Contrary to other women who invent complicated stories—a rich childhood, serious liaisons which, however, had ended badly—she remained a closed book.

Dronsart was not even able to make any deductions from clues, signs, scattered indications which, when put together, would make sense, begin to take shape. He learnt nothing, could not even put his finger on one single detail. No remark slipped out, no word which would act as a key to open the door to the clearer corridors, the great halls of certainty. There are words which can suddenly reveal what kind of childhood one had, and what loves. Had she grown up in Paris or in the country? What had her love life been like? She had certainly had liaisons, she wasn't a virgin. But how far had it gone? With whom? And with what sort of lovers? It ought to be possible to piece them together, since most men have expressions, habits derived from their professions. And women immediately pick them up. But Nel had retained no trace of anyone, of anything. It seemed to Dronsart that she started with him, as if he himself had created her in the golden Eden of the old gardens that October evening. Nel! She was his Nel. She had taken the name for him. And that evening she had become dead to her real name, to her past and all the rest.

They were happy. Nel, pale and delicate, fell ill with pneumonia. It was serious from the start. The night-light that shone through her white complexion dimmed, her skin took on the dull, leaden tone of snow about to melt. Nel's life was in danger. At that Dronsart became concerned about the mystery that had never been cleared up, the continuing enigma of her identity. She was young, she doubtless had parents who were still alive. And a husband she had left, perhaps. Ought they not to be informed? Who knows whether she herself, during these last days, when one goes over one's life, whether she wasn't thinking about seeing them again without daring to say so? Dronsart decided to ask her.

'Wouldn't you like to have your mother here to look after you? Is there anyone you'd like to see?'

'Oh! Does that mean I'm going to die?' Nel exclaimed, with a heart-rending cry.

Without another word, she turned to the wall. For a long time Dronsart heard her crying under the blankets.

Not until the evening did she speak again. 'Tell me I'm going to get better! That I'll live! We were so happy!' Adding, reproachfully, 'You were asking questions again.'

'Of course not, you misunderstood me.'

'What is it to you?' she said in almost solemn tones. 'Even if I do die, isn't it better like that? Our love will not have had a name, no other name but ours. I was Nel—that is to say myself—for you alone. And it will be the best one of your life. Do you remember how we would stop, in the museums where you used to take me, at portraits with the title: Unknown. And we dreamt for a long time. That will be my love and it will be all the sweeter for it...

Nel died. Dronsart, sobbing, inconsolable, knowing nothing about her, not even her real identity, could only offer the name of Nel, damp with tears, to the clerk in the registry office who was unhappy with that and demanded dates, age, family details.

For Dronsart did not know anything at all about the woman who had been his lover for two years. But, recalling their last conversation, he had her cross in the cemetery marked with the melancholy but true inscription: 'Unknown', as if cemeteries were truly museums as well, the museums of death.

The Dead Town

They had arrived in the dead town a few days previously. They had left Paris as abruptly as if they had been fleeing. Tired of all the misery of adultery—the secretiveness, the lies, the quick glances, the brief kisses—of which true love is ashamed, like a king having to dress as a beggar to be safe, they had suddenly come to a decision. Theirs was a noble passion and they would acknowledge it openly. She would leave her husband, he would leave his wife. They would refashion their destiny. And that is what they did.

They had chosen a dead town away up in the north, in the mist, which had been made fashionable through books and the enthusiasm of visitors. It seemed so distant and yet was so near. They had arrived after barely a day's journey by rail. Immediately Paris was far, far away. And the life they had left behind as well? Oh, the sudden change of perspective brought about by travel and absence! How different everything was here: the people in the streets, the houses, the colour of the air, the sky above the roofs, a low sky, very close, with moulded clouds, and which looked as if it had come out of a painting. A unique setting, a subtle atmosphere of silvery greys, the patina of centuries on the old walls—a shimmering marvel for the eyes of a painter. He had told himself that he would work there, in seclusion, transposing these incomparable townscapes. A virgin subject. And the fame being the painter of all that would bring!

The lovers had settled in an old hostelry on the Market Square, opposite the Belfry. They chose it for its great age, for the gable with crow-steps bordering the façade of pink bricks repointed with fresh white bands of plaster. And then they had read that Michelet, the great historian and writer, had stayed there sixty years ago. The man who had written, in *L'Amour* and *La Femme*, pages full of caresses, of flashes of insight, would be there, invisible, in the atmosphere round the mirrors, like a smiling presence, a guardian angel...

How sweet are the first days and weeks spent together! They were masters of their own destiny, they became aware of themselves, they became aware of the town. It was intoxicating yet at the same time solemn.

The days passed by monotonously, but is true happiness not monotonous? They walked along the quais, where lifeless water was dreaming. They sometimes looked at themselves, from up on a bridge, in the water of the canals. Empty water where there was nothing but the two of them... Their faces were beside each other, but very pale, very far off, the reflection adding distance, like absence or memory. Mirrored there, they looked so sad! It was as if they were distressed at the thought of being already reduced to a reflection, a transient image that was wavering and about to sink to the bottom.

A great melancholy was hanging in the air, giving their love a more languid, more tender feeling. It was like the love one feels before a separation, it was like love in a country where there is a war, in a town where epidemics are raging. A strong love, from feeling close to death. Here death reigned, it was as if the town were the Museum of Death. Every day he thought he was going to get down to work, but what was the point of creating a living work in this silence in which everything was decomposing? He had responded with ecstatic admiration to the works of the Primitives preserved there: triptychs of the Annunciation and the Crucifixion, reliquaries with medallions as exquisite as miniatures, portraits of the kneeling donors on the wings—defining masterpieces of the old painters whose fingers, like those of priests, touched God. They had painted—the way we pray.

What can one do after them? The futility of any effort appeared. And also the delusion of fame, the swift passing of the days, the cruelty of life, which shows less pity towards people than towards things, all these painted faces still intact while the faces of flesh and bone had turned into some anonymous mud, some imperceptible dust.

The lovers spent their days taking slow walks. Sometimes they went into one of the churches, but there, too, the obsession with death resurfaced. The floor was covered with large funerary slabs, the tombs of bishops, of churchwardens, of famous parishioners, whose names, titles, dates of birth or death had gradually been eroded by the steps of the centuries. And they had the impression that their love was walking amid death.

Even during the nights, their nights punctuated by unending kisses, they were sometimes irritated by the carillon, which sounded every quarter of an hour from the top of the belfry opposite. A slow, indistinct jingling which seemed to come from far, far away, from the depths of childhood, from the depths of the ages. It was like a dead bouquet falling, an autumn of sound shedding its leaves over the town... The lovers listened, uneasy about something, though they couldn't say what. They stopped their kisses. Was it the devout town objecting to their love? And were these hours of ecstasy, during which they were more alive than ever, a provocation to death, which held sway over the town? Once the carillon had fallen silent their lips sought each other again hesitantly and for a while their kisses had a taste of dead ashes.

To them the carillon seemed like the disheartening proximity of death...

The woman was wearying of it. She was the one who had had the idea of going there. All lovers desire solitude in order to possess each other more completely. They create for each other a new universe inhabited by the two of them alone. But these two had not reckoned on death, which immediately made its presence felt here. Yes, their love was walking on dead ground. Everything was ceaselessly dying in the dead town. The woman, sophisticated Parisian that she was and instilled with a taste for perfume, had a refined appreciation of scents, a subtly educated sense of smell.

Here everything smelt of death. The centuries-old walls along the quais sweated—the salty smell of old tears. The ancient façades with their damp patches made one think of a poisonous tattoo. In the churches a stench of dampness hung in the air, of stale incense, of faded altar cloths in a sacristy cupboard the key of which has been lost for hundreds of years. The smell of death spread equally round all the districts of the town, as if coffins containing mummies had been opened somewhere—or the old tomb of the dead centuries reopened.

The woman suffered from this persistent smell which each day took away a little more of her zest. Especially since her lover also seemed to gradually detach himself from her and from everything. Their kisses became less frequent, the carillon no longer bothered them at night. They slept without clasping each other, their love lying between them, already cold and motionless, like the water of the canals between the stone embankments. Seeing him bored and with nothing to occupy him, she said, 'Why don't you do some work?'

'Tomorrow.'

He always said, 'Tomorrow.' He made plans, chose a good place, started to sketch something out, then stopped, put things off again. He did not feel in the mood, he who had thought he could work so well here, who had initially been filled with enthusiasm for these combinations of water, trees and towers beneath a silver sky, unique. To capture that light! To be the painter of this dead town as Turner was of Venice.

An Impressionist ideal and truly modern! That was what he had thought at first. How was it that, after having admired, adored the Primitives of the Flemish race, he had come to fall little by little under their spell, their influence, the longer he stayed? The colours on his palette grew darker, as if the shadow of all the dead fell across it. The gestures in his designs became stiff. He also started to paint Virgins, men weighing out gold, donors. He imitated the old masters and it was not long before all he was doing was copying them. He felt that here any other art but theirs was a sacrilege. Ridiculous to want to be oneself in the midst of them! A feeble candle burning in the sun. The painter was vanquished. Here the dead had triumphed once more. The dead town had caused his new art to wither as it had withered his new love.

The lovers felt more and more out of sorts with themselves and with everything. The man seemed to have changed so much. He was morose, bored. He did not complain but his eyes were bathed in regret. His former life was taking hold of him again. When his companion occasionally spoke about Paris, he would quickly interrupt her, as if to remove a temptation which he would not be able to continue to resist. A great coldness developed between them, they seemed detached from each other, almost indifferent. And to think that during the months of their secret affair they had so much desired to belong to each other, entirely, day and night. But nothing specific had happened, neither was disillusioned with the other during this joint existence, this absolute intimacy. No clash, either, nor any quarrel.

What had happened to them? Now the man went out all the time, and always alone. He was out for whole afternoons, came back late, went to bed without a word. One evening he announced that he had received a letter from Paris. His art dealer had written that there was some important business to be done and he would have to deal with it in person.

'Don't lie! You don't love me any more and you want to leave me,' his lover said in resigned tones, not darkened by any feeling of rancour, simply sad, as one is when faced with the inevitable.

The man did not attempt to deny it: 'Yes! It's the fault of this town.'

The woman, pale and mournful, agreed: 'It's not our fault. Death is stronger than Love here.'

They remained silent for a long time, thinking of the dead town and their dead passion, of themselves, who felt as if they had committed suicide at the height of their love and now, resuscitated like Lazarus, had to start living again—each going their own way.

Out of Season

That autumn Mme Cantin was surprised and enraptured by what went on inside her. It was a mild October, still warm, with an end-of-season charm. In the park surrounding her house, a kind of castle on the outskirts of a small industrial town, some of the chestnut trees had blossomed again. What a joy is a large garden, restoring one to nature, to grass, leaves, water, to all those elemental things! At that particular moment Mme Cantin felt in harmony with her garden. She had just reached forty, but instead of ushering in decline and the approach of winter, this birthday signalled a revitalisation. Remontant roses were blooming anew on the bushes and she felt a parallel flowering in her heart. The evening skies were bright red; was that what had given her lips their rosy hue, as if she had painted them with the rejuvenated ruby rays of the setting sun? The garden was resplendent. The inconstant clouds played in the pond, changing their gowns, the ripe apples in the trees were radiant, flushed with the red tints of children's bare skin.

During those days Mme Cantin spent all her time in the garden, waiting, with an impatience she had completely forgotten, for evening to fall, the time when her husband would come home. Years ago she had watched for his return like that, impatiently, even feverishly. How time had dragged without him! Every day, without fail! Every morning he went to his factory, which was the source of their wealth but which definitely took up too much of his time. Newly wed—and having married entirely for love—she would have liked to keep him to herself, all the time, every minute of the day. To make his absence shorter, she would go to meet him, almost to the factory itself. Later on she had resigned herself to his absence, quietened down, still loving her husband, but with a more restrained affection and one which had to be shared out, for she now had three daughters, three girls, all the same, with the same fair complexion, the same blond hair, honey or amber blond. They were so alike that, after having called the first one Rose, because it seemed impossible not to call her that, the two others were given the related names of Rosine and Rosette. They were like three consecutive hours of the same day. They always went walking together, arms round each other's waist. And they had the fancy of always being dressed alike, with clothes of the same colour and style, hats with the same shape and flowers. As they walked side by side it was impossible to say where the one ended and the other began...

Mme Cantin had loved her daughters with a passionate affection, which meant there was all the less for her husband. And then, suddenly, she had started to feel the sap flowing again, a renewed inner turmoil in his presence, a reawakened thrill of the flesh, an impatience at having to wait for him in the evening, as she had during the first months of their marriage. That coincided with his absence abroad for a fortnight connected with a railway for which his factory was to supply the materials. It felt like a hundred years. At night she couldn't get to sleep in the empty bed... On his return this revived love burst forth and now it burnt, persisted, lingered like the autumnal warmth in the garden. She was aware of the complicity of the season, she was in collusion with the reflowering roses. The intoxication of renewal! It was the joy of lovers making up after a quarrel, coming together again after a long absence. But are we not always parting a little? We part the moment we loosen our embrace. But of all new beginnings the most intoxicating are those which roll back the years, give us delusions about our age, reviving the initial ardor between two people, the electricity of the senses we thought had been dulled, the mystery of our own being which is like the dark, arousing bed-chamber of Love. Once again Mme Cantin experienced the profound thrills, the constant discoveries of love, which lasts as long as it keeps being renewed...

All of a sudden, after twenty years of marriage, it was like a love affair, her husband was astonished, enraptured and could not get enough of her. Their October was like a second spring. There was even the prospect of a remontant rose to add to the family, a late rose of this lascivious and colluding autumn, one more rose after Rose, Rosine, Rosette, an unexpected bloom to be added—how?—to the close-knit and harmonious bouquet of the three girls already in their teens.

At first Mme Cantin was uncertain, but it quickly became obvious to her and soon it would be obvious to others. She wondered about her daughters and was concerned. She asked her husband, 'Will we have to tell them?'

At the thought of her daughters Mme Cantin was overcome with a kind of shamefaced embarrassment. She started to blush in their presence, as if what had happened to her were abnormal, as if it were shameful, at her age, to have yielded to such sensual delights. Love has its proper season. Like a young girl hardly into puberty and already pregnant faltering in the face of her mother's propriety, she felt uneasy in the face of her daughters' innocence. She kept going over the same question, unable to decide whether it would be better to keep quiet about it until the very end or not.

132

'They'll understand without having to be told,' her husband said.

'Who knows?' Mme Cantin replied. 'They're still so innocent!'

Still innocent indeed. None of them had been sent away to boarding school, they had all been taught at home, under their mother's eye, by governesses and private tutors. No contact, none of the mixing that can initiate and pollute young minds, they had been brought up in an atmosphere of reserve and religion. They possessed the modesty of the young roses they resembled and from which their names had been taken: Rose, Rosine, Rosette, so similar to each other that it would have been impossible to tell them apart if it had not been for the difference in age. Rose was eighteen, Rosine sixteen and Rosette, the youngest, only thirteen. Nevertheless they were all similar, dressed in the same clothes, all with the blond hair which seemed to be three parts of the same tresses. They were of the same character too, open, affectionate, sensitive. When they walked, they always went with their arms round each other's waists. A single group and in such harmony! It was as if they were propelled by the same spring, were the three sails of the same ship. They were always in agreement, had the same tastes, liked the same music, kept everything in common.

During those months Mme Cantin was in torment not knowing whether her daughters suspected anything, for her condition had become obvious and now she blushed even more in her daughters' presence. She wore loose bathrobes all the time, thought up enfolding gestures, as if it were something shameful she had to conceal, a sin which she did not want to disturb their innocence. Yes, they were innocent, but innocence is not the same as ignorance. Did they know something of the mystery of the sexes and of motherhood?

Were they aware of the event that was approaching? Or ought they to be told? Rosette, who was only thirteen, would certainly know nothing of the matter, but the eldest, Rose, was eighteen. Could she have retained her artless ignorance? When out on walks, even among her relations, she must have often seen pregnant women and wondered about them. After all, pregnancy is highly conspicuous. The second, Rosine, was sixteen. At that age children's minds are active, so she too must be aware of what it meant. Moreover the three sisters were so similar, so close, they thought the same way and told each other everything. Rose must know and therefore Rosine as well. But did that mean that the youngest, Rosette, must also know? For some reason she could not explain their mother found the idea upsetting. Why? That she should disturb the calm of her little Rosette, with her soul that had not yet lost its bloom, her modesty intact! And since she would not be able to understand everything, she would feel a sort of disgust, a horror of her mother, as if she had discovered that her parents lacked modesty, connected with those shameful parts of the body to which she herself closed her eyes so that she would not see them when she changed her underwear.

Mme Cantin was seriously concerned, especially since at that time Rosette seemed troubled, sad, paler than usual. She asked her, 'What's wrong?' She asked her sisters. They all said it was nothing, but their mother sensed that the approaching event was involved, was disturbing their young minds. But to what extent? Once again she wanted to reveal everything and suggested that to her husband.

'No, no. Let things take their course. Everything will sort itself out.'

One evening Mme Cantin was sitting in an arbour outside in the garden. After the heat of the day it was pleasant under the green vault, which provided coolness and a sombre light, the light of an eclipse, of a church nave. The foliage was so dense, she was almost invisible there. Stretched out in a cane chair, she was daydreaming, wearied by the growing weight of her love, her love of the previous autumn, born in this garden, her remontant rose in collusion with those of the garden. She thought of the birth, which was fast approaching. She thought of her daughters, above all of Rosette, whose anxiety, which she could not bring herself to clear up and which was doubtless connected with her condition, was getting worse. All at once she saw her three daughters appear at the end of the avenue, in a row with their arms around each other's waist as usual. It was a like a wave, breaking a little more at one side because of the height of the eldest girl. They were walking up and down the path, talking in confidential tones. They did not see their mother who, hoping she might learn something, kept quiet, hidden by the compact foliage of the arbour. She caught some scraps of their conversation. Rosette, the youngest, was crying. She said, 'But I do! I'm sure Mama's ill, you just won't tell me. She's seriously ill. I've seen her tummy. And it makes her look ugly. I don't want Mama to look ugly...'

Rosette burst out sobbing. Rose, the eldest, comforted her: 'But she's not, I tell you. It's nothing. Just wait a few weeks and Mama will be like she used to be. But above all don't talk to her about it.'

Rosine, the middle one, backed her up: 'Rose's right. Stop crying, Rosette.'

And the harmonious trio walked up and down with the cohesive motion of a wave rolling, breaking and reforming.

In the arbour Mme Cantin, silent, holding her breath, cried tears of joy, of wonder, of delight. So Rose and Rosine knew, Rosette did not. And how scrupulously the two older ones had kept the mystery from their younger sister. Now Mme Cantin blushed even more in front of her daughters, being aware that they knew.

She withdrew, devoted herself to Rosette, who suspected nothing.

Fortunately the event came sooner than expected, cutting short the mother's daily torment, the feeling of shame before her older daughters, a psychological unease, a physical embarrassment which grew with each day.

But as soon as the new-born baby had arrived, she had no trouble showing it to her three daughters, talking about it, expressing her rapture, her pride in it. The child had taken away all the sin.

'Who is it?'

The extraordinary news came as a real bombshell to this northern village: 'Ursula, the simpleton, is pregnant!'

The tale went from door to door. The majority refused to believe it. What, the village idiot? That poor, grotesque creature with the dazed expression, the misshapen body, more of an animal than a woman, shambling along like a bear as she wandered all day round the streets and fields? Impossible. No man could desire her. But people insisted it was true. What a business! There was no end of laughter, of obscene jokes. Neighbours went to ask each other. Out in the street people greeted each other with merry cries:

'Was it the work of the Holy Ghost?'

'No, the devil's work, surely?'

In fact the whole village immediately, at the very same moment, had the same thought: 'Who is it?' With some it was simple curiosity, with others spitefulness. It was a perfect topic for idle and malignant tongues to feed on. A mystery to be solved, and a mystery with a touch of the scandalous about it at that! A murky affair, certainly, and one in which everyone could entertain the hope of compromising their enemy, of spreading suspicion and anonymous allegations about him! The pleasure of hurting people and getting one's own back! The vicious pleasure of washing dirty linen in public! Monotonous evenings by the fireside enlivened by juicy items of gossip.

Who is it? The whole village was asking the same question,

'Who is it?'

some not from a taste for scandal but out of genuine outrage at such a shameful event. The guilty man must be found and punished by the general censure for he was guilty and despicable into the bargain, since after all the poor idiot had the defenceless simplicity of a child and should enjoy the same kind of inviolability as things of nature...

After high mass, groups formed in the square and talked for a long time amid whispers, laughter, dirty jokes and shocked expressions. All at once someone cried out, 'Look! She's coming.'

And indeed, there she was coming down the street leading to the church, an indistinct figure all in grey amid the garish surroundings of the low cottages with their geranium-red tiles, their white-and-green shutters.

This time everyone looked at her more attentively, in the light of what they now knew. Her body was misshapen, one hip higher, giving her the gait of a sailor unused to dry land and a slightly drunken air. Her squashed nose and the nervous tic jerking her mouth all the time, as if on a string, gave her face the look of an animal. In this rough sketch of a face only her large, clear, moist eyes retained a vestige of humanity, as if destiny had taken pity. She was leaning on the stick she always carried, which she would brandish when the village children threw stones at her—as they would at a bird—as if she were about to chase and beat them, but then, lacking the strength, she would continue with her feeble steps, constantly stumbling in the tangled web of her intentions. That day her limp was more pronounced than ever because she had lost one of her shoes. She had lost it as she came without noticing. It made her seem even more incomplete...

As she approached there were ripples in the groups, laughs, calls, quite a commotion. Everyone surveyed her with inquisitive looks. And indeed, her threadbare dress did seem shorter at the front, revealing her non-matching feet...

Still no one could really believe it. She really was too horrible. One old woman remarked with a knowing air, 'It's a tumour.' A man left one of the groups, saying, 'I'll go and talk to her.'

They saw Ursula stop in her tracks, seized with fear. The invisible string jerked her face in a most ugly grimace. Her body trembled with the epileptic trembling of a bear.

The man said, 'Come on now, is it true? Tell me who the father is... I'll give you some money.'

She didn't reply. He tried again: 'Who is it?' But the simpleton didn't seem to understand, her eyes alone, with their vestige of humanity, were imploring. She pulled away from the questioner, as if she had to break free from shackles, and went off, uncertain, her caricature of a body standing out against the purple shadow of the square in the sunlit village while the children interrupted their games to throw stones at her again, as they would at a bird.

A few months later Ursula, the simpleton, did actually give birth. Until then people laughed at her, sceptical, only seeing this unlikely maternity as a subject for jibes, jokes, crude stories and smutty remarks. When they saw the child the crowd's natural human instinct was aroused—and their sense of pity. The neighbours hurried round, the whole village arrived, cramming the little house where she lived with old Marie Nimy, an aunt over seventy who had taken her in. Everyone wanted to see the child. All the villagers made a contribution towards the baby clothes. The poor little innocent! So sweet and rosy-cheeked. There was nothing to see at that point except that it was physically perfectly normal. No deformity; but that can appear later, when it starts to grow, as had happened with its mother. What was regrettable was that she paid no attention to the child. Not a glimmer had lit up the darkness of her brain, awakening the maternal instinct. They showed her the child, gave it to her to kiss, tried to put it in her lap, but they had to pick it up again quickly. She would have pushed it away from her like a bundle of rags. What dreadful heredity, almost inevitable with such a mother. One day the poor child, sleeping there, would doubtless be like her. Oh, was it not a crime to give birth to a child that could only become a monster? Who was the guilty man? Now it was no longer a joke. People were outraged. They felt a kind of remorse. Simple-mindedness is a kind of childhood and you could say the woman lived under the protection of the village. She was the weakest of weaker vessels and someone had taken advantage of that.

Who is it? The question kept returning, tormenting everyone. They searched, they asked around in the whole neighbourhood. They questioned Marie Nimy. Did they have male visitors? What acquaintances did she have? Had Ursula not given any hints, anything that could be followed up? They questioned her, but she hardly understood what they were asking. Words had no meaning for her. They were simply a muddle of noises that reached her mind like the wordless sounds of the wind in the trees or of water lapping against the arches of a bridge.

She tried to imitate the sound of the words. They showed her the child and then, hoping to arouse an association of ideas in the chaos of her mind, asked, 'Who is it?' She responded with inarticulate cries, that had nothing human about them, were nothing but the sounds made by some object: the grating of a key, the tick-tock of a clock, the gurgling of a bottle...

But they needed to know.

They went to see the priest. 'It's a crime,' he said, speaking in a tone he would have adopted if someone had been murdered in the region. But he thought the damage was irreparable, the perpetrator impossible to find. The people went on at him to intervene, to help them in their search. The priest was a mystic, a visionary, human affairs were of little interest to him. He repeated, 'It's a great misfortune,' but already his voice seemed distant, his eyes on other things.

The general curiosity, on the other hand, did not give up so quickly. In the village there was now a whole crowd of people constantly searching, questioning, following up leads, checking information, setting up an enquiry. One fact had been established: it wasn't some stranger who happened to be passing, for none had been reported for the time in question. That meant it was a man from the village who was keeping quiet, secretly laughing at the public concern, cowardly and despicable... but still they couldn't find him.

One day Ursula herself almost solved the mystery. She had been seen suddenly going towards a young man who was passing with a visionary, ecstatic look on her face; she reached out towards him, tried to take his hands, made an attempt at a smile, hinted at lewd gestures—as if she recognised him. Immediately the incident was common knowledge. The wretch! They spied on him, During the following days Ursula repeated her performance, becoming bolder, provocative. She followed him, waited outside his house. The villagers were jubilant. At last they had discovered the secret. They decided to demonstrate their displeasure by serenading the culprit with a cacophony of pots and pans and lids. However, just at that moment Ursula turned her attention towards someone else, also a young man, whom she watched out for and followed with her pathetic lewd gesticulations. Then, not long after, there was another, then another and another. Ursula assailed all the men with her provocative gestures. She stared at them, tried to touch them, laughed her sad, broken laugh, like one coming from a face reflected in a pool into which stones have been thrown.

A strange phenomenon. A partial lifting of her inner darkness. She remained unmoved by motherhood but she had felt love; she didn't understand about the child, but she had tasted man. And now, with her female instinct awakened, she went to those who were young and handsome...

The village abandoned its search. The simpleton was a simpleton, there was no point in attaching any importance to her dumb show. All the more so because at that point the child died. Immediately it was as if nothing had happened. He had been the cause of their outrage, now things were back to normal. Ursula's liveliness only lasted a short time. She hardly went out any more, slipped back into apathy, into an almost animal life, apart from her large, sad eyes which had something human about them but were of no use since they had not even seen her lover of one night of deepest darkness...

And later on, when some neighbour would insist on asking her aunt, old Marie Nimy, about the event—'Who is it?'—with a shake of the head she would reply in her hoarse voice, 'It was no one's bastard.'

Love and Death

One Sunday afternoon, at the house of the old lawyer where one could chat at one's ease, where, as Gautier says, one could enjoy the pleasure of immersing oneself in masculine talk, the conversation came round to the subject of love. A banal topic. It was the spring that prompted it. It rose up from the frail garden, still recovering from winter, came in through the half-open windows: the scent of the first lilac, of the new shoots, of the watered soil, which smells good. And then we had just been talking about a dramatic item in the newspaper reporting once again the death of two lovers who had committed suicide together.

The novelist, de Hornes, responded by declaring, in his voice that was always slightly husky, as if to go with his grey eyes, the grey of ashes smouldering with faint flames, 'No one has ever truly loved if, at some point or other, he has never had the idea of dying with his mistress.'

'How deuced romantic!' the old lawyer exclaimed. In fact, his outlook was too close to the eighteenth century for him to be able to comprehend the tragic depths passion can reach. For himself, he had never been more than a collector, as they used to say, for whom a woman has the same value as a precious curio. But Valmy was there and balked at de Hornes' claim for other reasons.

'On the contrary, it's very scientific,' he broke in. 'All we have there is a general law of physics, a natural phenomenon of depression, depression which becomes excessive when one is too much in love and which weak lovers are unable to overcome. Basically it's the *animal triste* of the Romans.'

Valmy was a Darwinist and larded his theories with difficult words from science with, moreover, a quasi-religious fervour, eyes blazing, authoritarian gestures, arms stretched out like posts indicating directions.

But de Hornes refused to be put down by this positivist self-confidence. He went on, 'All the same, you must agree that this sadness after lovemaking is not simply the weariness that follows exertion but, rather, something like the melancholy at the end of anything enjoyable, that is something psychological...'

'Agreed,' said Valmy, 'but in that case it is due to the vague awareness of the trap which is love. One can understand the selfishness of Nature, only thinking of herself, of reproduction. That is, man feels duped by a mirage which ceases with the cessation of desire, and he is sorrowful.'

'There is more,' de Hornes insisted, 'this sadness is not purely a matter of instinct, it is often very conscious, entirely cerebral.'

Then he returned to his theme: 'If so many lovers feel the desire to die and more and more die each day, while still in love, it is because love and death are linked by analogies, by underground passages, and communicate. One leads to the other. The one makes the other more acute, more intense. There is no doubt that death is a great stimulant of love. How else can one explain the habit village lovers have of leaning against the cemetery wall to take each others' hands and lips? And it goes all the way from simple souls to the highest minds. Did not Michelet take his fiancée, the love of his later days, the remontant rose of his October days, to the hill on which

144

the Père-Lachaise is situated, knowing he could more easily talk to her of love among the graves and of eternity in the face of death?

'There are many other indications that support this idea. A murderer hurries to the whore immediately after he has committed his crime—he needs sensual pleasure because he has seen death... And the taste we have for women in mourning, is that not a similar sign? Not in the case of blondes, who are more beautiful in their black dresses and so ethereally loving, but of all those in the livery of mourning, which makes them arousing, tempting because of the sense of death around them and within them, which one dreams of mingling with love...'

The old lawyer was listening with interest, raising his handsome, pale head, which looked as if it had been moulded out of moonlight. Now it seemed even paler in the twilight of the day's end. The room was growing darker in the corners, less because night was falling than because of the gloom flowing in from those dubious regions of the mind our conversation had opened up.

Despite the serious talk, our lips had taken on a feverish hue. We were all remembering. De Hornes, with his dreamy voice, had called up ghosts. Within himself each one of us reawakened his loves from the past, moments long gone, distant kisses. Within himself each had a sense of dead leaves, old graves, the dried-up residue of tears. And yet spring was rising through the half-open windows, the scents from the frail garden were importunate...

Valmy, sticking to his natural explanation, replied, 'These are over-refined decadent fancies, they have nothing to do with instinct or something innate, as you believe. Primitive people know nothing of such subtleties and would despise them. Savages are unaware of them.'

Love and Death

'Yet as early as the Song of Songs,' de Hornes observed, 'love is associated with death: "for love is strong as death; jealousy is cruel as the grave." Moreover,' he added, 'one day I had an experience which confirmed the mysterious analogies uniting them. It's a strange story from my past which gives me a kind of chill every time I think of it.

'When I was twenty-five I had a mistress whom I loved above all for her pale complexion, her air of a beauty struck by tragedy, her slow steps, which always made her look as if she were walking among ruins. She lived alone, separated from her brutal husband. One day her aunt—who had brought her up, like a second mother—came with her sister, who was younger than her. We didn't see each other for several days. Eventually she sent me a telegram asking me to come to the hotel where her relations were staying. Her aunt was ill and she had stayed with her, could not leave her. But now she wanted to see me, to build up her reserves of courage.

'I went, but hardly were we together than a great cry was heard and she rushed off. One moment later it was her own voice crying out, calling, calling me, screaming. There is no mistaking the arrival of death. I understood and dashed off after her. On the bed: a woman, already with the pallor of death on her, the whites of her eyes showing, her mouth open, like a dark hole the departure of the soul had left black, and her arms slumped along her sides, as if in surrender. You can visualise the death: in the hotel, alone, instantaneous, with neither help nor farewells. In the hours that followed my mistress seemed to me more noble and grave than ever: she was almost as pale, with the air of a statue standing by a dead woman. Her younger sister, devastated, was silently crying in an armchair. After paying our last respects, someone had to go and carry out the various tasks and obligations connected with the death:

registry office, mourning clothes, relations to be informed. My mistress insisted on looking after these things herself; there was comfort for her in these family duties, which she did not want to leave to anyone else. She just asked me to stay with her younger sister, who felt afraid in the hotel suite with the dead body.

'I spent the twilight hours with her. And this is the strange, incredible part of this story. I tried to console the orphaned girl as best I could. But words are no use, she felt that herself and didn't speak. She was sitting close beside me in the room next to the one we didn't dare go back into again... I was going to light the lamp, but she said, 'No, there's no point. Don't leave me.' And she took my hands, as if to thank me for taking pity on them, for coming to their aid in their loss, for seeing that there was someone there sharing in their grief. Crying made her look like a child and I wiped away her silent tears. For a moment her hands squeezed mine. I certainly had no idea of doing her any harm. She came close to me, leant against my shoulder as if her head had become too heavy from the added weight of all the tears that were coming. Unintentionally some of our hair touched, mingled. What was the terrible madness that suddenly gripped us? There, in the hotel suite invaded by death, with the corpse nearby, her face touched my face... Then I felt her lips placed, as if involuntarily, against my lips, like the mouth of a bottle. Love? Impossible at a moment like that, too sacrilegious, too monstrous! Moreover, night having fallen, merged with the darkness, I was a vague figure, an anonymous form, hardly human. I realised it was nothing to do with me personally. I provided an immediate and necessary way of helping her to blot out her overwhelming grief.

'She had wanted the kiss as a narcotic, like morphine or opium, a sure drug... In that way she did find forgetfulness, she was no longer aware, she drifted off, she let herself go in the sweet pleasure of self-abandon... What a terrible scene! I was trembling, I felt ashamed. Did I have no part in it at all?

'During the days that followed I didn't dare look at her. But she was calm, showed no sign of remorse, and once more became the enigmatic figure I had known before on the rare occasions when I had met her with her sister. All the time afterwards she displayed the same profound indifference towards me, as if nothing had happened. And, indeed, nothing had happened. Once more love and death had found themselves acting in collusion, linked by their mysterious corridors... It was the proximity of death that was the stimulant...'

De Hornes paused for a moment. The others remained silent. It was as if the little room had expanded as twilight obliterated all detail...

De Hornes went on, speaking quickly, as if to get this memory over with, the long story which had taken too strong a hold on our attention:

'That's the way it is, always, everywhere: the word love and the word death end up coming together as if they were the two sides of a mountain. And that's why I said, "No one has ever truly loved if, at some point or other, he has never had the idea of dying with his mistress," because the point at which the two sides meet is the summit, the plateau, the culminating moment. The moment when love and death are one...'

De Hornes fell silent. The gleam faded from his grey eyes, the grey of ashes. No one spoke.

The old lawyer seemed to be meditating. This acceptance of a mystery was anathema to his clear mind, his inductive method. In condescending tones Valmy broke the silence, 'Oh yes, nature has its forces, its occult purposes.'

No one else spoke. Each one of us was thinking of life,

of his own life. The scents of eternal spring were coming up from the frail garden. But now the little room had become sad, completely overtaken by night... and Darkness and Silence combined; and it seemed as if it were Love and Death coming together once more.

Consecrated Boxwood

One year there was great consternation on Palm Sunday in one of the quiet beguinages of Flanders. The hour of the high mass was approaching. The bell in its openwork turret was ringing, so faintly it seemed to drift on the wind like a wisp of sound. A few of the faithful from the surrounding district were already arriving, gentle old women whose woollen mantles also swung like bells. Beguines were starting to leave their little convents, heading for the service.

But in the church the sacristan, Sister Dorothée-des-Anges, was pacing up and down with increasing anxiety. That morning the florist of the district, with whom she had dealt for so long, had not delivered the usual supply of boxwood. And yet she had expressly gone to see him a week previously in order to remind him. He couldn't have forgotten. What had happened? He or someone in his family must have suffered a misfortune. Sister Dorothée-des-Anges was frustrated, having given up hope that he would come. Yet it was absolutely essential they had branches of boxwood for the ritual ceremony that day and also to supply the beguinage and the faithful of the neighbourhood, who were relying on it.

So she made a drastic decision and hurried over to the mother house in one of the corners of the enclosure where the Grand Mistress resided. She told her that they had been let down and the situation was now urgent, there was only one solution: to send out an order to all the houses to cut the ornamental boxwood that was a traditional feature of the little gardens where, glossy and docile, it fringes the paths, forms the initials of patron saints, Sacred Hearts pierced by a green sword.

The initial response was one of real distress, for the beguines are very attached to their pretty gardens, that satisfy their taste for ingenious arrangements—their design corresponds to the designs of their lace. They too consist of rosettes, slender transitions, open or half-open corollas. Parallel work, meticulous and fragile both: their lace is like white windows encrusted with frost patterns; their little gardens are coloured windows...

They quickly resigned themselves to the loss, out of obedience and in order not to displease God. In the House of the Eight Beatitudes, in the House of the Love of God, in all the important houses of the community the order was carried out without delay. The plants were cut off level with the soil and piled into wicker baskets from the workroom. The harvest from each little garden was sparse, but enough to make it look entirely bare. Then beguines recalled a similar sacrifice they themselves had accepted on the day when their hair was cut off and it made their little gardens even more dear to them. It was as if on that day they too had taken holy orders.

Now while all the big houses had immediately sacrificed their boxwood finery, there was a long discussion in a very small house, the House of Mercy that stood at the end of one of the twisting alleys. It was one of the best-kept, dazzling in its cleanliness. The brass on the door shone like that on the stern of the barges on the canals; the widows gleamed, their muslin curtains so fresh they looked like the veils of girls taking their first communion; the plaster pointing of the pink brickwork made white stripes across the façade. It was an abode so patiently cared for it was almost unreal, a little dwelling place preserved under glass which doubtless vanished into thin air every time someone passed by. A fairy-tale house, a dream house. You were amazed whenever a beguine appeared at one of the windows. It was less like seeing a cornet, than catching a glimpse of a soul in flight, linen wings on the way to heaven...

The miracle of such care was due to Sister Monique, who lived there with just two other beguines. With only three of them, perfect tidiness and cleanliness was possible. Sister Monique was scrupulous in this and had managed to instil the taste in her two younger companions. The least hint of dust offended her as if it were a venial sin of the furniture. She was even more strongly opposed to disorder, to neglect that led to dirt or untidiness, to anything that disturbed the immutable order that had given the house a look of eternity, as if it were already outside time, with no trace of corporeality, of life. When, therefore, they too received the command to cut down the box in the garden for the ceremony of Palm Sunday, Sister Monique was initially devastated. But the next minute she had made a decision. She could never bring herself to simply go and destroy her little garden, which was as charming, well-kept, correct, fixed, one might say, as the rest of their house. She quickly found specious arguments against it. She only had a small amount of box, making a Sacred Heart in the central bed. What difference would these few branches make to the great pile gathered from the other gardens of the beguinage? It would be like placing a candle among the stars in the sky. She would not comply—no one would be the worse off. No one would notice. So she told the other two beguines of her firm intention, urging them to keep it absolutely secret. In that way their garden would be saved from the massacre! She had put too much care into ceaseless digging, raking, sowing, planting, watering for someone to require her to lay instant waste to it. It truly was too cruel. It was like asking her to mutilate her own child. And Sister Monique, as she went to mass, full of indignation, felt she could see on the other grass-green doors a cross of blood, as there had been in Judaea for the massacre of the Innocents...

At mass it was very moving. Each of the beguines, in their long white veils, was given a branch of consecrated box from the officiating priest as they entered in procession. They rejoiced, holding the one branch given back from the garden they had sacrificed, happy at the gift to God, and the gift to others, for members of the congregation joined in the procession, gentle old men, women in their mantles, the faithful of the district into whose hands their gardens were scattered. The joy of giving! The priest of the beguinage based his sermon on it. He spoke movingly of the grace of God who had thus put their goodwill to the test. And all had responded to the divine appeal, none of the beguines had shirked their duty, they had all sacrificed the boxwood from their gardens. A sacrifice that was as beautiful as it was symbolic! This Sacred Heart of greenery was also their own heart. And God requires us always to act in that way: to create an everlasting heart for ourselves and then to give it to others!

Sister Monique listened to the sermon with growing agitation. 'None of the beguines had shirked their duty!' Of course the priest didn't know, but God did. All at once she realised how mean a sin she had committed. Beforehand you find good reasons for yourself, you delude yourself with pretexts and lies. It is a ruse of the Fiend who colours over sin, disguising the ugliness of its face. Now she realised what she had done. In the first place she had disobeyed the order of her superior, the Grand Mistress, which was bad enough, but above all she had behaved badly towards God. She had refused to give up the box from her garden to deck the altars. How shameful! To haggle with the Church, to cheat God! Sister Monique saw herself as having committed a great sin. Now the branch of consecrated boxwood she had been given by the officiating priest during the procession burnt her hand with the agony of remorse. She did not dare keep it, take it home with her. She went to place it on the altar to the Virgin Mary, an offering of atonement among the bouquets and silver-gilt vases. She lit a thin taper, that too in atonement, on the wrought-iron hearse with its constant flickering light.

Back at the little House of Mercy the sight of the preserved garden, where the boxwood Sacred Heart still wound its green curves, only increased Sister Monique's anxiety. Over the next few days she was going to have to hide from all eyes, keep her door closed to all untimely visits, not allow the secret hidden behind it to come to light. She only hoped the two young beguines who lived with her would not let anything slip! She bombarded her companions with instructions, to their great discontent, since they had protested from the start, not wanting to be disobedient. Now they were annoyed at having to share the responsibility and the remorse. A bitter dispute ensued in the course of which they reproached her harshly. Sister Monique reproached herself all the more. Even her garden was no consolation. She looked on it with horror as her tempter, the cause and occasion of her fall. The Fiend had decked himself out in flowers to sully her soul. It was the snake from the Garden of Eden winding its way round her little garden in the form of a Sacred Heart, with all its boxwood scales.

Sister Monique, who was old and had long suffered from a weak heart, spent that Sunday deeply perturbed. She considered herself to be in a state of mortal sin. She also believed her reputation was ruined, for her disobedience would become known throughout the beguinage. She went to bed that evening in great discomfort. And when she did not get up at her usual time the next morning her two companions found her dead in her bed.

When the Grand Mistress came in with the priest and the other beguines, whom they had quickly called to help, they were astounded to see the Sacred Heart still intact in the garden.

'Sister Monique didn't give her boxwood!'

The news caused a great scandal. Above all the sacristan, Sister Dorothée-des-Anges, was filled with indignation. All the beguines crossed themselves. This sudden death was a punishment from God. Each one repeated in a horrified voice, 'She didn't give her boxwood!' They were sure she was damned, or at least condemned to a long period in purgatory.

While her body had been laid out on the little bed with pale lilac cambric curtains and a copper crucifix placed in her hands, they needed a branch of boxwood standing in holy water to put beside her on the chest of drawers, according to custom. Sister Monique had not dared bring her own branch back from the church. One by one each of her fellow beguines was asked, to give theirs. They all refused, out of fear or a feeling of rancour towards the one God had punished. In the end they had to resign themselves to taking a branch from sister Monique's own little garden, which they put in a glass of water beside the body. She had wanted to leave her own garden untouched—but it was touched by death! And the place where they cut into the boxwood, in the Sacred Heart, suddenly looked like a gaping wound, the inevitable wound from which sister Monique had died.

Pride

Old Count Jean Adornes had died, causing great sorrow throughout Flanders. In all the dependent farms the women made their children with their corn-coloured hair kneel down before the plaster statuette of the Madonna, white against the blue-washed walls, and say an *Ave* for his soul. The bells rang out from village to village, as if drawing trails of sadness through the air, black trails that joined up. His vassals brought all the hollyhocks and sunflowers from their gardens and branches in blossom from their orchards to the castle gates.

Count Adornes was popular throughout the land. There was not a single blot sullying his noble life, he was kind, charitable, chaste, loyal to God and to his name. An illustrious name that had shone brightly since the dark beginnings of recorded history. It was one of his ancestors who had distinguished himself in the first Crusade, taken part in the capture of Jerusalem and, in memory of that, built the chapel in Bruges which bears the name of the holy city and in which he is buried. And his fortified castle of Saint-André is already mentioned in papers in the archives going back to 1200 and 1220. One part still existed, in dressed stone of enormous thickness, with a square tower and a round tower. Circling it was a moat twenty feet deep with drawbridges which, at this moment, were not lowered, as if they had been raised on the divine entry of death.

But the drawbridges would be lowered again for the day of

his funeral, which was to take place the following Sunday, so that everyone in the land could attend. The wrought-iron gates would be opened as would all the outside doors and the doors to all the rooms. The castle would belong to the people. For before the cortege could leave, the centuries-old ceremony, which was still observed, had to be gone through. This was the judging of the deceased in the great hall of the castle, which was thus turned into a court of justice. An age-old tradition to which all the lords of the land of Flanders had submitted since the earliest times; so sure they were of the righteousness of their life that they allowed their subjects to discuss it. All their relatives gathered in council with their vassals, tenants, farmers, servants, and this council became a tribunal with pleas for or against the deceased, whose body was waiting in the chapel. The statements were gathered impartially. If the sum total of good was greater than that of evil the coffin was borne with due deference and praise to the family vault; if, on the other hand, the memory of the deceased was tainted by some more serious sin, especially if he had not obeyed the laws of religion scrupulously, if he had caused some scandal, he was carried off without ceremony, almost in secret, to some isolated pit where he was left and forgotten.

A strange custom! Popular justice seen as equal to divine justice. A whole life weighed in the eyes of the masses as if in the scales of a balance.

The day arrived. The widow of the old Count, Lady Ursule Adornes de Borlant, wanted a ceremony full of pomp, worthy of the deceased. Since she was artistically inclined and liked music, she had a large organ installed, whose reverent cadences with their hint of eternity would be appropriate, filling the judgment hall with the solemnity of death, like a

157

catafalque of sound. All the doors were opened and the crowd entered. Because of all the hollyhocks, all the sunflowers from the gardens, because of all the branches full of blossom from the orchards, which were still constantly arriving at the castle, it had less the gloomy melancholy of mourning than the bright adornment of Rogation Days. The widow wept all the more at the sight of this cheerful blossom, but the tears she wept were less bitter. She was the one who had wanted this poetic ceremonial. And, following her wish, before the solemn voices which, when called upon, were going to speak about the deceased, praising or questioning his life, children's voices would open the proceedings with sweet motets, angelic hymns that happened to have been learnt by the village choirs. Lady Ursule de Borlant wept abundant but sweeter tears as she listened to these sweet voices, voices like those of her own children when they were small, in the early years of her marriage. Years of love that had come to an end. Her husband was at rest. Oh, those pure soprano voices! She felt that they were going to her deceased husband resting in the chapel, in his closed coffin, that they would refresh him in his sleep, perhaps thirsty from the fires of purgatory.

The singing ceased, the organ folded away its heavy velvet. In the silence that followed a voice called on the crowd gathered there, his next of kin, his relations, his friends, his servants, his vassals, his tenant farmers, all the people of the land who had been invited, to speak out: to praise the deceased or question his life, criticise his deeds, reveal some lapse or sin that had remained hidden. No one dared speak, there was a solemn silence which seemed to grow more and more profound, like a vault into which the deceased was already sinking, lower and lower. So in order to encourage the judgment of the people, Lord Borlant, the late Count's brother-in-law and close friend, set out a kind of questionnaire listing the deadly sins which sum up the great transgressions against God, against one's fellows and against oneself. 'Pride?' At that all the people whispered, 'No! No!' The murmur was infectious, unanimous, like corn bending in the same direction as the wind passes.

He continued the list of deadly sins: 'Avarice?' The rumble of the same negative spread through the throng—everyone was thinking of the Count's charity.

'Lust?' In an admirable expression of the people's instinct, the crowd turned towards Ursule de Borlant, the sole love of the deceased Count, his companion in a chaste and fruitful marriage. They all bowed towards her, it was solemn and moving. She gave a cry in which there was sorrow, but also pride. No other woman had tempted him. Faithful to his wife, as she had been faithful to her husband, they had both respected the holy sacrament of marriage.

He finished the list: 'Envy? Gluttony? Wrath? Sloth?' each followed by a murmur of denial, the corn waving again.

Then there was profound silence. A slight noise of breathing could be heard, of mourning veils and crepe crackling when someone moved, of the trees waving in the park that came in through the open doors, as did the sound of the crowd outside, for there was only room for some of those who had come. Then the venerable Jean Biscop, who had been the village priest for almost fifty years, came forward and stood in the space that had been left empty. He seemed hesitant, embarrassed, kept his eyes fixed on the floor, never had he looked sadder. He started to speak in the tone he used from the pulpit when he had to censure some scandal that had happened in the parish.

'It is true that Count Jean Adornes, Baron of the Holy Roman Empire, Lord of Saint-André, was a mighty and charitable lord, and many were his virtues in the eyes of his fellow men and of God. He was indeed unacquainted with avarice, lust, envy, gluttony, wrath and sloth. As for pride, it is also true that no one was simpler, friendlier in his dealings with humble folk... But, my brethren, I owe it to my calling, to my conscience and to the honesty of this public judgment, which is one of the oldest and most precious customs of Flanders, to admit before all of you gathered here that he was not simple in his dealings with God. He committed the sin of pride, and his pride went as far as sacrilege. I alone know this—and God. I am therefore obliged to reveal this to you, since I represent God in this court of justice. I hesitated, but I feel it is my duty. Even when the Count was alive I wanted to oppose him, but I did not dare. I was a coward, I was a partner in his sin of pride. In revealing it today I am almost making a public confession... Count Jean Adornes was filled with pride towards God. Infatuated with his nobility, his titles, his coats of arms he was determined to assert them even in his devotions.

'Just imagine: not content with having the foremost place in the choir of our church, and the prie-dieu like a throne, which I granted him out of weakness and in response to his generosity, he carried his aristocratic demands even farther. And this was the sacrilege in which, alas, I was all too involved. Even as far as holy communion was concerned, that egalitarian sacrament instituted by Our Lord's great goodness, he was determined to distinguish himself from the common faithful. Could Jean Adornes, direct descendant of the one who took part in the first Crusade and rests in the Chapel of Jerusalem in Bruges, which he established, take communion in the same way as the other parishioners? He gave me a seal with his ancient coat of arms, that is the count's crown and the emblem of a battlemented tower surrounded by ornamental leaves.

'He ordered me to impress his seal on the host that was

for him every time he took communion. The sin of pride. A sacrilege of which I am ashamed. God in the host was not enough for him, he had to add his coat of arms to God! Oh, how those emblazoned and consecrated hosts often burnt my fingers as I presented them to the proud lips of the Count! He would look at it to make sure that the whiteness of unleavened bread was embossed with his escutcheon. Only then did he deign to receive it—though in full faith, I have to admit. But I suffered. And doubtless Jesus suffered too. I felt I could see Him, His face captive behind the lacework design of the count's crown, as if on the battlements of a prison. He was entangled in all those emblems cluttering up the host that hardly left any room for Him. I am sure Jesus was less present in those hosts than in the others...'

Those who heard this were dumbfounded. Yes, the sin of pride, of pride in a name which had dared to bracket itself with the very name of God! A sacrilege for which the deceased had to be made to atone by a penance which was the essence of humility.

Then, following the custom, the priest, the noble lords and the people decided that he would not be laid to rest in the family vault. So the following day Count Jean Adornes, Baron of the Holy Roman Empire, Lord of Saint-André, was taken, without pomp or ceremony, to the village graveyard where he was lowered into the earth—and no stone marked the anonymous grave.

The Canons

The bishop was dead. His end was as resolute as his life. On his deathbed, after having received extreme unction, he searched his conscience and prepared himself to meet God, Monseigneur Prat remained firm, clear of mind and almost jovial in the presence of the stern deans and canons, his servants and faithful valet, who were crying. He was remembering his life. He thanked Providence; he had had a good life, beautiful and eventful, it had matched his dream. He had fought great fights with his crozier, against unbelievers and free-thinkers, his works had covered the diocese with a goodly crop of monasteries, convents and almshouses. He had enjoyed popularity, almost fame. Now he was recalling all the details of his career as bishop and deputy, his visits to Paris, the nice 'bachelor flat' he had there, in the Faubourg Saint-Germain, and his successful speeches, his days of triumph addressing the Chamber, where his priestly hands quivered like wings, where his pale hands soared like a dove, the dove of the Holy Spirit, over the assembled deputies, like a bird soaring over the sea.

Monseigneur Prat remembered. Carried away, he exulted, essayed once more some oratorical gestures. Sitting up in his bed, close to expiring, propped up by cushions, he remained cheerful, joyful, almost combative right to the end. He was holding a large ivory crucifix and he was playing with it, making it slip between his fingers, throwing it, catching it, swinging it in a thousand unconscious games, like a fidgety person with a paper-knife reading a new book.

The stern canons were shocked. They would have liked to take the holy crucifix away from the irreverent dying man. But they did not dare. He had persistently treated them in an authoritarian manner and even at death's door he still inspired fear. His eyes lit up for the last time. He spoke, very lucidly and quickly, making thousands of recommendations. With a malicious smile suggesting a perfidy they did not as yet understand, he gestured the archdeacon to approach and said, gasping for breath, 'Will... There... Desk drawer... Holograph... No lawyer... Tomorrow... Read to canons tomorrow!' And he died immediately, as if, having delivered this message, all that was left was to take refuge in death. And the large crucifix slipped out of his hand, dropping onto his chest, where it also seemed to fall asleep, like a friend on his friend's breast.

There was great mourning among the people, who loved Monseigneur Prat for his generosity, his outspokenness, his resoluteness. In the town and in the whole diocese there was genuinely heartfelt sorrow. The bells of the parish churches rang out, drawing black paths through the air which seemed to be crowded with mourners.

In the bishop's palace, in the grand chamber, the embalmed body of Monseigneur Prat, dressed in his bishop's robes, was seated in state on a kind of vast dais lit by candles and surrounded by relays of seminarists for the vigil. They, too, loved their bishop. He had captured the hearts and minds of these young priests, being himself as carefree as the young, free from doubt, trusting in chance and in God. The canons, on the other hand, had lived in a state of perpetual conflict with their bishop. It annoyed them to see him behave in such an unconsidered manner, too daring, too plain-spoken, with no idea of diplomacy, not calculating his ideas any more than his spending. In what state would they find the diocesan administration?

The next day, in accordance with the last wishes of His Lordship, the archdeacon gathered the cathedral chapter in the committee room to read to them Monseigneur Prat's will, that had indeed been found in the drawer of his desk which he had indicated.

From the very first lines they were dumbfounded. The bishop confessed that his finances were encumbered with debt. His will was a balance sheet, and a very precise one considering how disorganised they thought he had been. He had committed himself too deeply, to many different projects: there were architects' bills for old folks' homes, orphanages and new monasteries; loans for the diocesan schools, which had cost so much during the period of the struggle against secular education. On the other side he set out his personal fortune of three hundred thousand francs, which he left to pay off a little of the sums owed; then he listed his furniture, the things he owned in that 'bachelor flat' on the Faubourg Saint-German.

The archdeacon paused in his reading of the will. His voice was quivering, he was choking with anger, and with shame at the sudden revelation of such a state of affairs.

'Scandalous!' It was one of the youngest canons who had ventured to speak, expressing in that single word what everyone felt.

The others grew bolder, one exclamation was followed by another:

'He deceived us!'
'He was a fool!'
'A scoundrel!'

'Debts of two million!'

'What can we do?'

'Bankrupt! A diocese going bankrupt!'

The archdeacon went on reading the will: 'In my Paris apartment there are some objects of value the sale of which will increase the sum of my estate: rare books in my library, including first editions of Bossuet, Racine, Ronsard; and my works of art, my pictures—I have two drawings by La Tour, which are worth a good thirty thousand francs, and a Delacroix which must be worth the same.'

At that there was an angry outburst among the canons: 'A Delacroix! He bought paintings and didn't pay the masons! Was it for that that he collected from the faithful, fleeced them!' Once more the exclamations poured out, but the archdeacon was already continuing: 'I have ten pastoral rings, some with valuable stones. They will suffice to pay—out of my estate but without them being mentioned in the accounts—my publisher who has brought out the ten volumes of my collected parliamentary speeches, pastoral letters and sermons.'

The exclamations from the assembled canons were even louder; a laugh ran round the gathering, like foam on the waves:

'His complete works!'

'Not one copy of which has been sold.'

'All plagiarised!'

'Yes! From Lacordaire, from Bourdaloue...'

All the rancour, the long hostility burst out. The red wine of ambition, long bottled up before the bishop's authority and turned to gall and vinegar, streamed out of their hearts, filling a pool of hatred. A stunned silence followed, then the sneers started up again:

'And his rings to pay for his books!'

'Ten rings, like a woman!'

'Presents, perhaps...'

'Who knows what kind of life he led, up there in Paris?' said one of the oldest canons, the dean of the chapter, the one who had expected to be given charge of the See when Monseigneur Prat had been appointed in his place following goodness knows what intrigues and compromises behind closed doors with ministers of the Republic! 'An apartment! Should not a holy bishop rather stay in a convent, with a priest or, at most, in a house for ecclesiastics... But an apartment!'

'A bachelor flat!' the youngest canon exclaimed in a shrill voice.

'Yes, like a man-about-town!'

'Who knows, perhaps he entertained women there?'

'That's where the money from the diocese will have gone...'

At that there was a veritable storm of cries, laughs, curses, sarcastic remarks, a hullaballoo filling the committee room, battering the walls, threatening to break down the doors and engulf Monseigneur Prat lying in state in the adjoining room. The archdeacon, a cautious hypocrite, signalled the frenzied gathering to be silent: 'Careful!' And the canons quietened down to conceal their consternation from the seminarists who, duped by their bishop, were keeping their tearful vigil round him.

Monseigneur Prat was given a grandiose funeral. All the powers that be were there, singing the praises of that great political and religious figure: a bishop and a deputy, he had above all been a great patriot. The people mourned his passing as well, blocking the streets where the lamps, lit and swathed in crepe, evoked golden hearts, birds of light come down from heaven and in mourning as well. And the outburst of emotion when the body passed, still on the high dais from the bishop's palace! He sat there, his face uncovered, looking up at the sky from which the sound of the bells poured down. An impassive face, suffused less with the beauty of death than with the calm of eternity. It was Monseigneur Prat himself, become a marble statue. How moving to see their dead bishop, his face uncovered, proceed from the palace to the cathedral. It was the custom in that region, still attached to the old traditions. The funeral mass was celebrated with great pomp. The organ deployed its black velvet, a thousand candles sparkled, their wax showing the pallor of death; and at the absolution the aspergillum sprinkled cold drops over the congregation in a last scattering of tears.

After that the cathedral was cleared and the heavy doors locked. The sextons brought the bishop's coffin and placed it in front of the dais which, during the mass, had served as a catafalque. And, as was also traditional, the canons prepared for the deposition of the body of his lordship.

It was they and they alone who were to perform this final office. They lifted up the body and transferred it to the coffin, then withdrew the cushions it was resting on in order to lay it out flat. At that moment there was a remarkable sight. The bishop remained upright, unsupported and yet steady, in a sitting position. His body had stiffened in the posture in which it had been quickly placed at the moment of death. Now there was no way of straightening it out, of flattening the angle, of opening out the terrifying compasses he made. He stayed sitting up in his coffin. They tried to lower him, to lay him flat. He resisted them. The canons stared at each other, dumbfounded. Soon they were furious, he still seemed to be mocking them, defying them...

Then the youngest of the canons plucked up his courage, pressed his hands against the dead bishop's chest, grasped him by the shoulders and forced him back until his shoulder blades were touching the floor of the coffin, as a wrestler does with a defeated opponent. A sinister cracking sound could be heard. At that all the canons joined in. They attacked the corpse, stretching it, bumping it, flattening it on the floor of the lead coffin, forcing back its clasped hands. Without bending down, the archdeacon dropped the gold crozier, which hit the dead man in the face. Finally they lowered the lid with a great crash, but since it refused to close properly, since the torso and head still stuck up because the body had been in a vertical position for so long, the canons, with stifled laughs, their rancour appeased, making one great, concerted effort to weigh down the coffin, sat on it.